PAUL TEMPLE
TWO PLAYS
FOR RADIO
VOLUME 2

Francis Durbridge

WILLIAMS & WHITING

Cover design by Timo Schroeder

9781915887658

Williams & Whiting (Publishers)
15 Chestnut Grove, Hurstpierpoint,
West Sussex, BN6 9SS

Titles by Francis Durbridge published by Williams & Whiting

Murder At The Weekend – the rediscovered newspaper
serials and short stories

Also published by Williams & Whiting:

Francis Durbridge: The Complete Guide
By Melvyn Barnes

Titles by Francis Durbridge to be published by Williams &
Whiting
A Case For Sexton Blake – radio serial
They Knew Too Much – magazine serial

INTRODUCTION

Francis Durbridge (1912-98) was a prolific writer of sketches, stories and plays for BBC radio from 1933. They were mostly light entertainments, including libretti for musical comedies, but a talent for crime fiction became evident in his early radio plays *Murder in the Midlands* (1934) and *Murder in the Embassy* (1937). The *Radio Times* (11 February 1938) mentioned that Durbridge had by then written some one hundred radio pieces, and Charles Hatton commented in *Radio Pictorial* (28 October 1938) that "He is one of the very few people in this country who have succeeded in making a living by writing for the BBC."

Durbridge pursued his radio career by writing plays and serials for many years, using his own name and occasionally the pseudonyms Frank Cromwell, Nicholas Vane and Lewis Middleton Harvey, but his principal claim to fame was the creation of the novelist/detective Paul Temple and his wife Steve. The radio serial *Send for Paul Temple* (1938) resulted in listeners bombarding the BBC with over 7,000 requests for more, and Durbridge responded later the same year with *Paul Temple and the Front Page Men*. Then from 1939 to 1968 there were another twenty-six Temple cases, of which seven were new productions of earlier serials, maintaining Durbridge's impressive UK and European reputation.

The Temples also appeared in a syndicated newspaper strip with a daily run from December 1950 to May 1971, and from 1969 to 1971 in a television series (although this was not written by Durbridge). But it was in 1952, while continuing to write for radio, that Durbridge embarked on a succession of BBC television serials that attracted huge viewing figures until 1980. Then from 1971 in the UK, and even earlier in Germany, he carved a reputation for cleverly crafted stage plays that are still produced by professional and amateur companies today.

The radio exploits of the Temples were mostly broadcast as eight-episode serials, although two of them ran for six episodes and one was a lengthy ten episodes. There were also some one-off Paul Temple plays, beginning with an abridged production of the original serial *Send for Paul Temple* on 13 October 1941 (one hour). Then an abridged production of the third serial *News of Paul Temple* followed on 5 July 1944 (one hour), and later there were two original plays - *Mr and Mrs Paul Temple* (21 November 1947, forty-five minutes) and *Paul Temple and Steve Again* (8 April 1953, one hour).

This series of books published by Williams & Whiting sets out, by transcribing Durbridge's surviving typescripts, to present as complete an oeuvre as possible. Already published, as well as most of the Paul Temple serials, are the above-mentioned plays *Mr and Mrs Paul Temple* and *Paul Temple and Steve Again* in the volume *Paul Temple – Two Plays for Radio*, and now we have the abridged one-hour versions of the serials *Send for Paul Temple* and *News of Paul Temple*. When the first of these was broadcast Durbridge wrote an article called "Potting Paul Temple" for the *Radio Times* (10 October 1941), concerning the problems he had to overcome when condensing a serial of over three hours into a one-hour play, which was a process he had clearly found equally or even more demanding than writing the original.

Inevitably, for each of these one-hour versions, the original cast of characters had to be reduced and some characters and their plotlines were deleted. Secondly, although not so inevitable, the original actors were all replaced. In *Send for Paul Temple* (13 October 1941), compared with the original serial (8 April – 27 May 1938),

Carl Bernard replaced Hugh Morton as Temple, Thea Holme replaced Bernadette Hodgson as Steve, Cecil Trouncer replaced Lester Mudditt as Sir Graham Forbes, Ivan Samson replaced E. Stuart Vinden as Dr Milton, Grizelda Hervey replaced Cecily Gay as Diana Thornley, Amy Veness replaced Courtney Hope as Miss Parchment, Edgar Norfolk replaced William Hughes as Pryce, Ivor Barnard replaced Vincent Curran as Chief Insp Dale, Arthur Young replaced Denis Folwell as Horace Daley, William Trent replaced Cedric Johnson as Insp Merritt, Allan Jeayes replaced Butts Marchant as Dixie, Antony Holles replaced Hal Bryant as Skid Tyler, and Cyril Gardiner replaced Duncan Blythe as Supt Harvey.

Then in *News of Paul Temple* (5 July 1944), compared with the original serial (13 November – 18 December 1939), Richard Williams replaced Hugh Morton as Temple, Lucille Lisle replaced Bernadette Hodgson as Steve, Laidman Browne replaced Lester Mudditt as Sir Graham Forbes, Grizelda Hervey replaced Diana Morrison as Iris Archer, Molly Rankin replaced Mona Harrison as Mrs Moffat, Alexander Sarner replaced Bruce Winston as Laurence van Draper, Lewis Stringer replaced Maurice Denham as Rex Bryant, Cyril Gardiner replaced Cyril Nash as Major Guest, Gladys Young replaced Gwen Lewis as Mrs Weston, Preston Lockwood replaced Dick Francis as Ernie Weston, Basil Jones replaced Ben Wright as David Lindsay, Frank Cochrane replaced Ewart Scott as Ben Collins, and Arthur Ridley replaced Dick Francis as the Newspaper Editor.

It is worth mentioning that both of the original radio serials were novelised, with *Send for Paul Temple* co-authored by John Thewes (John Long, June 1938) and *News of Paul Temple* co-authored by Charles Hatton (John Long, May 1940). These two novels have been regularly reprinted and also marketed as audiobooks, while the complete scripts of the original full-length radio serials are also included in this Williams & Whiting series.

So how can the essential elements of Francis Durbridge be summarised? Whether for radio or television, with every serial he devised a complicated mystery with the focus of suspicion switching between characters. It was typical for a teasing cliff-hanger to leave his audience in suspense at the end of each episode, and he introduced into his plots everyday objects and motifs with a puzzling significance. Ask any Durbridge fan to explain his popularity, and all will surely mention these factors.

His reputation has endured, and his name has become a gilt-edged trademark.

Melvyn Barnes
Author of *Francis Durbridge: The Complete Guide* (Williams & Whiting, 2018)

This book reproduces Francis Durbridge's original scripts together with the list of characters and actors of the BBC programmes on the dates mentioned, but the eventual broadcasts might have edited Durbridge's script in respect of scenes, dialogue and character names.

SEND FOR
PAUL TEMPLE

An abridged version of the radio serial
presented as a complete play
By FRANCIS DURBRIDGE
Broadcast on BBC Radio
13 October 1941
CAST:

Paul Temple . . . . .Carl Bernard
Steve Trent . . . . Thea Holme
Sir Graham Forbes . . . . Cecil Trouncer
Superintendent Harvey . . . . Cyril Gardiner
Chief Inspector Dale . . . . .Ivor Barnard
Inspector Merritt . . . . .William Trent
Dr Milton . . . . Ivan Samson
Diana Thornley . . . . .Grizelda Hervey
Pryce . . . . Edgar Norfolk
Skid Tyler . . . . Antony Holles
Dixie . . . . .Allan Jeayes
Horace Daley . . . . .Arthur Young
Miss Parchment . . . . .Amy Veness
Sergeant Leopold . . . . John Bryning

OPEN TO:

VOICE: The following is from the present edition of 'Who's Who' …
          "Paul Temple. Bramley Lodge, Bramley, Nr. Evesham. Educated at Rugby and Magdalen College, Oxford. Author of 'There is no Mystery,' a novel that attained phenomenal success in 1930. Son of Lieut. General Ian Temple, he was born in Ontario. Achieved considerable fame as a criminologist being responsible for the arrest of Tony Jilepi, Guy Grinman, and Tessa Juta. His play 'Dance Little Lady' was produced in 1929 at the Ambassadors Theatre and ran … for seven performances."

FADE IN of opening music.

Slowly FADE music.

VOICE: The Office of Sir Graham Forbes, Chief Commissioner of Police, New Scotland Yard.

A door opens.

LEOPOLD: Superintendent Harvey and Chief Inspector Dale, sir.

FORBES: Good! Let me have the map straight away, Sergeant.

LEOPOLD: Yes, sir.

FORBES: Come in, Dale! Come in, Harvey!

The door closes.

DALE: (*Briskly*) Good morning, Sir Graham!

FORBES: (*Tensely*) Well?

DALE: (*Quietly*) It's the same gang, sir. I'm afraid there's no question of it.

1

FORBES: (*Grimly*) T't! This makes the seventh robbery in two months! What did Merritt have to say?

DALE: (*Amused*) He's in a complete daze, poor devil! He's got some fancy sort of theory about a huge criminal organisation. I think Inspector Merritt has a rather theatrical imagination.

FORBES: M'm. Er … did you see the night watchman, Dale, before he died?

DALE: No, sir … but Harvey did.

FORBES: Well, Harvey?

HARVEY: (*Quietly*) He was pretty groggy when I saw him. The doctor wouldn't let me stay above a couple of minutes.

FORBES: Did he say anything?

HARVEY: Yes. Yes, as a matter of fact he did.

FORBES: Well … what did he say?

HARVEY: It was just as I was on the verge of leaving. He turned over on his side and mumbled a few words that sounded almost incoherent at the time. As a matter of fact, it wasn't until a minute or so later that I realised what he'd said …

FORBES: Well, what <u>did</u> he say?

HARVEY: (*Quietly*) He said … The Green Finger.

There is a slight pause.

DALE: The Green Finger …?

HARVEY: Yes.

DALE: (*Suddenly*) Sir Graham, do you believe the same as Inspector Merritt, that we <u>are</u> up against a definite criminal organisation?

FORBES: (*After a pause*) Yes. Yes, I do, Dale.

DALE: (*Significantly*) I suppose you've seen the newspapers?

2

FORBES: (*Impatiently*) Yes. Yes, I've seen them.
             (*Bitterly*) "Send for Paul Temple" ... "Why
             doesn't Scotland Yard send for Paul
             Temple?" ... They've even had placards out
             about the fellow. The press have been very
             irritating over this affair – very irritating.
DALE: (*Thoughtfully*) Paul Temple? Isn't he the
             novelist chap who helped us over the
             Tamworthy murder?
FORBES: Yes.
DALE: He's a friend of yours, isn't he, Harvey?
HARVEY: I know him ... yes.
FORBES: Temple is just an ordinary amateur
             criminologist. He had a great deal of luck
             over the Tamworthy affair and a great deal of
             excellent publicity for his novels.
HARVEY: (*Quietly*) I don't think Paul Temple exactly
             courted publicity, Sir Graham.
FORBES: Don't be a fool, Harvey, of course he did. All
             those amateurs thrive on publicity. Why, ever
             since this confounded business started people
             have been bombarding us with ...

The door opens.

FORBES: ... What is it, Sergeant?
LEOPOLD: The map, sir. Remember, you asked me to ...
FORBES: Oh, yes! Yes! Yes! Put it on the desk. Thank
             you.

The door closes.

There is a tiny pause.

FORBES: Now, gentlemen, you see this map? It's a map
             covering the exact area in which, so far, the
             criminals have confined their activities. You
             will see the towns which have already been
             affected. Gloucester, Leicester, Derby and

Birmingham. The map starts at Nottingham and comes as far south as Gloucester … covering in fact, the entire Midlands. (*After a slight pause, and with dramatic deliberation*) Gentlemen – somewhere in that area are the headquarters of the greatest criminal organisation in Europe. That organisation <u>must</u> be smashed!

FADE IN of music.

FADE DOWN music.
FADE IN of general laughter.

MILTON: So what did you say, Temple?
TEMPLE: I said: My dear Madam – the story may be hackneyed, the psychology may be warped, the characters may be unpleasant, but, By Timothy, the spelling's terrific!

They laugh.

MILTON: Well, personally I thoroughly enjoyed the novel. (*To DIANA*) Here's your coat, Diana.
TEMPLE: Allow me.
DIANA: Oh, thank you. (*After a tiny pause*) Mr Temple, what do you really think about these robberies one's been reading so much about? Do you think it's the work of an organised sort of … er … gang, or do you think …?
MILTON: (*Amused*) Oh, come on, Diana! Don't start troubling Mr Temple with a lot of newspaper nonsense!
DIANA: You know perfectly well he's been avoiding the subject all the evening!

They all laugh.
The door opens.

TEMPLE: (*Still laughing*) Yes, Pryce?

4

PRYCE: (*Quietly*) Superintendent Harvey of Scotland Yard would like to see you, sir.

The laughter dies down.

There is a tiny pause.

TEMPLE: (*Softly*) Superintendent Harvey …? (*Suddenly*) Yes, all right, Pryce. Show him into the drawing room.

PRYCE: Yes, sir.

TEMPLE: Will you excuse me?

MILTON: But, of course.

DIANA: Yes, of course – and thank you for a very lovely evening.

TEMPLE: Not at all. Miss Thornley and Dr Milton are leaving, Pryce.

PRYCE: Very good, sir.

There is a pause.

A door opens.

TEMPLE: Hello, Harvey! How are all the bright little boys at Scotland Yard?

HARVEY: (*Obviously very worried*) I don't mind telling you things are in a pretty serious condition. During the last two months nearly £50,000 worth of diamonds have been spirited away from under our very noses. And you can take it from me there's going to be bigger stuff than this, unless I'm very much mistaken.

TEMPLE: (*After a tiny pause*) Does Sir Graham know that you've … er … come to see me?

HARVEY: Well … er … as a matter of fact … er … old man … no. I thought that with your being in the actual district we might … er … well …

TEMPLE: Have an unofficial chat about the matter, is that it?

5

HARVEY: Er … yes. I'm sorry, Temple, but you know what Sir Graham feels like about outsiders.

TEMPLE: (*Quietly*) Tell me, Harvey, did you see the night watchman on the Birmingham job – the fellow who died?

HARVEY: Yes. His name was Rogers.

TEMPLE: Did he say anything before …

HARVEY: I only saw him for a few seconds, the doctor wouldn't let me stay any longer, but while I was there, he said, very quietly – The Green Finger … At the time I thought the poor devil was delirious, and talking nonsense. Now, however, I'm not so sure.

TEMPLE: M'm. (*Suddenly*) When did you come down from London?

HARVEY: This afternoon. I'm staying at The Little General for a night or two.

TEMPLE: The Little General? Oh, you mean the inn! Good heavens, don't be silly! You must stay here – there's tons of room. We'll run down into the village and get your things.

HARVEY: Look here, old boy, I don't want to put you to any trouble!

TEMPLE: (*Laughing*) By Timothy, you're the limit! I'll tell Pryce to get the car ready!

FADE IN of music.

CROSS FADE the music to the sound of a motor car slowly ticking over.

After a pause HORACE DALEY arrives. He is wildly excited.

HORACE: I – I say, mister, is that fellow a friend of yours, the chap who came into the inn about five minutes ago?

6

TEMPLE:	Yes. (*Alarmed*) Why … what's happened?
HORACE:	My Gawd, it's awful! It's awful!!!!
TEMPLE:	(*Sternly*) What's happened?!!!
HORACE:	He shot 'imself.
TEMPLE:	Shot … himself? No! No! No, that can't be true!
HORACE:	(*Wildly*) I tell you he's shot 'imself! Good God, man, d'you think I don't know when …
TEMPLE:	(*Quietly*) We'd better go inside.

The car door closes with a bang.

FADE the noise of the car.

PAUL TEMPLE is speaking on the telephone.

TEMPLE:	… Yes, I'm speaking from the inn, Sergeant … Well, it might be suicide … Yes, straight away … Oh, and bring Dr Thorne if you can get him … Oh, I see … Well, in that case, give Dr Milton a ring and tell him I've been in touch with you. Yes … yes, naturally …

TEMPLE replaces the receiver.

HORACE:	What d'you mean … might be suicide? You can see for …
TEMPLE:	(*Quietly, yet with authority*) Would you mind telling me exactly what happened?
HORACE:	No. No, of course not. This fellow comes in and says he's changed his mind about staying 'ere the night. He pops upstairs and brings his suitcase down. There it is, over there.
TEMPLE:	M'm … and then what?
HORACE:	Then he asks me if I could change a quid. I say "Yes" an' goes into the back parlour to get the money. When I gets back I sees him just like he is now … lying all twisted up like, with the gun in his 'and. (*Puzzled*) But why

7

didn't I 'ear the blinkin' shot? That's what I can't understand!

TEMPLE: (*Quietly*) The gun was fitted with a silencer.

HORACE: Ooo ... he did 'imself in in style, didn't he?

TEMPLE: Is there anyone staying here at the moment?

HORACE: Yes. An old dame who calls herself Miss Parchment. She arrived yesterday afternoon. Says she's on a walking tour of the Vale of Evesham. Don't look much like a hiker to me, though.

TEMPLE: I think you'd better fetch Miss Parchment down. I'd like to have a word with her.

HORACE: What do we want 'er for?

TEMPLE: The Sergeant will insist on seeing her, so there's no reason she shouldn't be brought down right away.

HORACE: (*After a tiny pause*) All right. If you say so, guv'nor.

TEMPLE: And you'd better tell her what's happened. We don't want her fainting or anything like that.

HORACE: If you ask me, she'll pass right out!

A door closes.

There is a slight pause.

TEMPLE is quite obviously taking stock of his surroundings.

He notices the till on the bar counter and suddenly decides to examine its contents.

The drawer of the till is opened and closed.

HORACE returns.

TEMPLE: You've been quick!

HORACE: Yes.

TEMPLE: (*After a slight pause*) Where's Miss Parchment?

8

HORACE: She'll be down in a minute.

TEMPLE: Have you told her about …

HORACE: Yes. And would you believe it, she was as cool as a cucumber. Talk about some of us men being 'ard-boiled! Why, if you … (*Suddenly*) Hello! 'Ere she is!

There is a slight pause.

TEMPLE: Miss Parchment?

MISS P: Yes.

MISS PARCHMENT is an elderly spinster.

TEMPLE: My name is Temple. Paul Temple. I'm most awfully sorry to disturb you at this time of the night but circumstances …

MISS P: Oh, please don't apologise, Mr Temple. Please don't apologise! Really, what a dreadful shock this must have been for you. Personally, I can never understand the mentality of anyone who commits suicide. It always seems to me that …

TEMPLE: What makes you so certain that this is suicide?

MISS P: What makes me so certain? But, surely it must be suicide! (*Brightly*) Unless of course Mr Daley shot him.

HORACE: (*Startled*) 'Ere none o' them ruddy insinuations! (*Suddenly*) And if it comes to that, why wasn't you in bed when I knocked on your door?

MISS P: (*Calmly*) Because, my dear Mr Daley, I was reading.

HORACE: (*With sarcasm*) Like to bet it was a murder story!

MISS P: You'd lose your bet, Mr Daley. (*With a steady voice*) It was a book on old English inns. I'm very interested in old English inns.

HORACE: Seems a funny thing to be interested in to me.

MISS P: I can assure you it's most engrossing. Why, do you realise that this particular inn is almost five hundred years old? Think of it! Five hundred years … and it wasn't always called The Little General, you know. Oh dear, no! Before that it had a most interesting name.

HORACE: (*Suddenly*) I say, can't – can't we cover him up or something till the Sergeant arrives? He looks 'orrible just laid there staring up at the ceiling!

TEMPLE: Yes. Yes, all right.

HORACE: I'll get a sheet from the linen cupboard. Won't be a minute.

A door closes.

A pause.

TEMPLE: (*Thoughtfully*) You say this inn wasn't always called The Little General?

MISS P: No.

TEMPLE: (*After a slight hesitation*) Then – what was it called?

MISS PARCHMENT commences to laugh. It is a slightly sinister laugh.

MISS P: A most intriguing title, Mr Temple. I'm sure you'll like it.

TEMPLE: Well?

MISS P: It was called – The Green Finger.

There is a long pause.

TEMPLE: (*Softly*) The Green Finger … (*Suddenly*) Are you sure of this?

MISS P:	Oh, quite sure. It's all in the book I'm reading, Mr Temple. A most interesting book.

A door opens.

HORACE:	(*Excitedly*) 'Ere's the Sergeant and Dr Milton, sir.

SERGEANT MORRISON and DR MILTON arrive.

SERGEANT:	(*Clearing his throat*) Good evening, Mr Temple! Evening, Daley!
HORACE:	Thank Gawd you've come, Sergeant, I was just about to …
SERGEANT:	(*With authority*) If you please, doctor!
MILTON:	(*After a tiny pause*) Could we have another light on, please, I can't … see … very clearly …

There is a pause.

SERGEANT:	Well, doctor?
MILTON:	(*Slowly*) He's been dead about a quarter of an hour I should say. He must have died instantly.
SERGEANT:	M'm. Er … M'm. Now I'd like a few details if you don't mind. Was the deceased a friend of yours, Mr Temple?
TEMPLE:	Well – not exactly what one would call a friend, Sergeant. I knew him … fairly well. His name is Harvey. Superintendent Harvey of Scotland Yard.
SERGEANT:	(*Amazed*) Superintendent Harvey! Oh, I really feel I ought to have a word with Inspector Merritt about this. Would you mind running me back to the station, Mr Temple?
TEMPLE:	No, of course not.

SERGEANT: I'm awfully sorry to keep you hanging about, Doctor, but I don't suppose we shall be very long. You see, Superintendent Harvey is rather a big noise, sir, so naturally …

MILTON: Only too glad to be of service, Sergeant. Think nothing of it!

SERGEANT: Thank you, sir. You can go to your room, Miss Parchment. I doubt whether the Inspector will want to see you tonight.

MISS P: Oh, thank you. Good night, Sergeant. Good night.

SERGEANT: Good night, Madam.

The door closes.

HORACE: I say, what the 'ell's going to happen to this fellow, we just can't leave 'im 'ere all the time.

SERGEANT: I'll attend to that, Daley! (*Pleasantly*) We'll be as quick as we can, Doctor.

MILTON: That's all right.

The door closes.

There is a long pause.

HORACE: (*Softly*) They've gone, Doc!

MILTON: (*Quietly*) Yes.

HORACE: I don't like it! I don't like it!

MILTON: Don't be a damned fool, Daley. Everything's turned out perfectly.

A pause.

HORACE: Have you had any more information about the Leamington job?

MILTON: Yes. It came through this morning.

HORACE: Well?

MILTON: We meet on … Tuesday.

HORACE: (*Surprised*) Tuesday! Phew! Here … or at your place?

MILTON: (*Quietly, yet dramatically*) Here … in Room 7.

FADE IN music.

FADE DOWN music.

PRYCE: (*Reading*) "In a locked room at the police station here tonight, Inspector Dale with Mr Paul Temple, the celebrated novelist, discussed the incidents leading up to the tragic suicide of Superintendent Harvey of Scotland Yard. It is believed …

TEMPLE: (*Finishing his breakfast*) Righto, Pryce!

PRYCE: Shall I read what the Daily Express says, sir?

TEMPLE: No. I think we'll leave that to the imagination. The marmalade, Pryce. (*After a slight pause*) Did anyone call yesterday while I was at the station with Inspector Dale?

PRYCE: Yes, sir. A young lady, sir. A newspaper reporter, sir. A very insistent young lady, sir. She simply wouldn't take "No" for an answer.

TEMPLE: (*Slightly amused*) Wouldn't she, Pryce?

PRYCE: A very pretty girl too, sir … if … er … I may say so.

TEMPLE: By all means say so, Pryce. A very pretty girl who wouldn't take "No" for an answer! M'm … M'm … Sounds interesting.

PRYCE: (*Thoughtfully*) Now what was the young lady's name? T't. T't. I made particular note of it because I thought it sounded rather silly for … Ah! … Steve … Steve Trent.

A bell is ringing.

PRYCE: It's the door, sir. Excuse me.

TEMPLE: It'll be Inspector Dale. You'd better show him in here.

A pause.

The sound of voices are heard in the background.

PRYCE is obviously rather excited.

The voices continue.

PRYCE: (*In the background*) I'm very sorry, Miss, but Mr Temple is out! (*Emphatically*) Oh, no I'm sorry, Miss. Really, Miss, I must ask you not to …

TEMPLE: What the devil is all this?

PRYCE: It's … It's the young lady, sir!

TEMPLE: Which young lady?

PRYCE: The … er … the reporter, sir.

TEMPLE: (*Amused*) Oh. Oh, I see.

STEVE: May I come in?

TEMPLE: Er … Yes, I think perhaps you'd better. (*A slight pause*) All right, Pryce, you can go.

PRYCE: Thank you, sir.

The door closes.

STEVE: He's very determined, isn't he?

TEMPLE: (*Surprised slightly by STEVE's manner*) Yes. Yes, very. (*Suddenly*) I say, look here … you can't come bursting into people's houses like this!

STEVE: I'm sorry but … (*Suddenly*) You are Paul Temple, aren't you?

TEMPLE: Yes.

STEVE: I tried to see you yesterday but your man said you were out.

TEMPLE: Well … we … what is it you wanted to see me about?

STEVE: (*Simply; after a tiny pause*) I need your help,
            Mr Temple. I need your help more than I've
            ever needed anything in my life before.

TEMPLE: I'm rather afraid I don't quite understand.

A pause.

STEVE: (*Very seriously*) Do you think Superintendent
            Harvey committed suicide?

TEMPLE: (*A shade amused*) My dear Miss Trent, I
            don't see that it makes a great deal of
            difference what I think!

STEVE: (*Suddenly: with emotion*) Please! Please,
            answer my question. Do you think
            Superintendent Harvey committed suicide?

A slight pause.

TEMPLE: (*Softly*) No, I think he was murdered.

STEVE: (*Suddenly, yet gently*) I knew it! I knew it! I
            knew they'd get him!

TEMPLE: By Timothy, you are a remarkable young
            woman! First of all you …

STEVE: (*Gently*) Gerald Harvey was … my brother.

TEMPLE: Your … brother!

STEVE: Yes. My real name is Harvey. Louise Harvey.
            I chose the name of Steve Trent partly for
            professional reasons … and … partly for
            another reason too. (*Suddenly*) Mr Temple,
            why do you think my brother came to see you
            … the night he was murdered?

TEMPLE: (*Thoughtfully*) I don't know. I'm not at all
            certain that he had any particular reason.

STEVE: He had a very good reason.

TEMPLE: Well?

STEVE: About eight years ago, Gerald was attached to
            what was then called the Service B.Y. It was
            a special branch of the Cape Town

15

Constabulary. At this particular time a very daring and successful gang of criminals were carrying out a series of raids on various jewellers within an area known as the Cape Town – Simonstown area. My brother and another officer named Bellman ... Sydney Bellman ... were in charge of the case. After months of investigation they discovered that the leader of the organisation was a man who called himself The Knave of Diamonds but whose real name was Max Lorraine.

STEVE pauses.

TEMPLE: Please do go on.

STEVE: From the very first moment when Gerald was put in charge of the Midlands case, he had an uneasy feeling at the back of his mind that he was up against Max Lorraine. I saw him a few days before he came up to see you, and he told me then that he was almost certain that Max Lorraine, alias The Knave of Diamonds, was the real influence behind the robberies which he and Inspector Dale were investigating. (*After a tiny pause*) I think he was a little worried ... and rather frightened.

TEMPLE: (*Thoughtfully*) Rather frightened? Then your brother must have known a great deal about this man.

STEVE: Yes, a great deal. (*Slowly*) And the day before he died he passed that information on to me.

TEMPLE: To you ...? That may mean danger. Great danger ... You realise that?

STEVE: (*Softly*) Yes.

A slight pause.

TEMPLE:	What is it that you know about Max Lorraine …?
STEVE:	(*Slowly*) I know that he has a small scar above the right elbow, that he smokes Russian cigarettes, and is devoted to a girl called … Ludmilla.
TEMPLE:	(*Thoughtfully*) Ludmilla … (*Suddenly*) Miss Trent, you said you wanted my help. You said, you wanted my help more than you've ever wanted anything in your life before. What did you mean by that?
STEVE:	I meant … that from now on, I want it to be Paul Temple versus Max Lorraine!!!

A slight pause.

TEMPLE commences to laugh – rather gently.

STEVE:	(*Surprised*) Why are you laughing?
TEMPLE:	I was just thinking of something Pryce said, before you arrived here.
STEVE:	Well?
TEMPLE:	He said: "you simply wouldn't take 'No' for an answer!!!!

FADE IN of music.

FADE DOWN music.

MILTON:	Now are you quite clear about the Leamington details, Dixie?
DIXIE:	Yes, I think so, Doc.
MILTON:	Good. (*Turning away*) Now, Skid … I want you to have a look at this map. You see Regent Street? That's where Diana will park the car. Now take a look at the corner. You can see the jewellers and the dress shop the moment you come round the bend. The Chief wants you to come round that corner at seven-

	forty precisely. You should reach the dress shop about seven forty-one. Then let it rip! Got that?
SKID:	Yeah, I got it all right.
HORACE:	Well, thank Gawd it's you on the lorry, Skid, an' not me!

A knock is heard.

It is followed by another knock.

There is a pause.

Two more knocks are heard.

SKID:	(*Quickly – nervously*) There's somebody at the panel!
MILTON:	(*Softly*) It's all right, Skid. It's only Diana.

A sliding door is opened.

DIANA:	Sorry I'm late. No, don't shut the panel.
MILTON:	(*Slowing closing the panel*) Why not?
DIANA:	(*Quietly*) The Chief's coming …
DIXIE:	(*Astonished*) You mean … the Knave is actually coming here …?
DIANA:	Yes. He's got the Birmingham money. It came through this morning.
SKID:	Blimey, that's quick work!
DIANA:	Have you given them the Leamington details?
MILTON:	Yes.
DIANA:	How do you feel about it, Skid? Think you can manage the smash all right?
SKID:	Yes … as easy as falling off a log.

A knock is heard on the panel.

HORACE:	(*Nervously*) What's that?
DIANA:	It's the Chief. I told you not to close the panel, Doc.

The panel is opened.

There is a slight pause.

MILTON:	Gentlemen, meet the Knave!

DIXIE: (*Astonished*) The Knave, but …

SKID: I thought you said the Chief was a …

HORACE: (*Amazed*) But – But this isn't the Knave … Why … Why …

MILTON: Surprised, gentlemen? Surprised?

MILTON commences to chuckle.

FADE IN of music.

FADE DOWN music.

TEMPLE: It was really decent of you, Steve, to come down from Town at a moment's notice like this. I hope it wasn't too inconvenient.

STEVE: No, of course not. (*Faintly amused*) But you haven't told me why you sent for me so suddenly.

TEMPLE: Well, Steve, because … Oh, by the way, I've decided to drop the Miss Trent.

STEVE: (*Laughing*) I rather gathered that.

TEMPLE: I sent for you because … because I want you to tell Sir Graham all you know about this man … Max Lorraine.

STEVE: (*Surprised*) But the police don't even believe my brother was murdered! Sir Graham telephoned this morning. I'm seeing him at three o'clock tomorrow afternoon.

The door opens.

PRYCE: I beg your pardon, sir.

TEMPLE: Yes, Pryce?

PRYCE: Inspector Merritt would like to see you, sir.

TEMPLE: Yes. Yes … ask him in here, Pryce.

STEVE: Merritt? Who's Merritt?

TEMPLE: (*Laughing*) Now don't tell me you've never heard of Inspector Charles Mortimer Merritt! Dear, oh dear, he would be flattered.

19

STEVE: Oh, I remember. He was helping Gerald and Inspector Dale over the jewel robberies. Is he a friend of yours?

TEMPLE: By Timothy, yes! Merritt and I get along like a house on fire.

STEVE: Have you know him long?

TEMPLE: About five or six years. He hasn't been in this country all that long. He was out in New Zealand for a little while – or somewhere like that. (*Amused*) If he wasn't so damned rude to his superiors they'd have had him at the Yard ages ago.

The door opens.

PRYCE: Inspector Merritt, sir.

TEMPLE: Hello, Charles! This is a pleasant surprise.

MERRITT: Just thought I'd drop in for a chat. Happened to be passing.

TEMPLE: Why, yes, of course. I don't think you know Miss Trent? Inspector Merritt.

STEVE: How do you do, Inspector?

MERRITT: How do you do, Miss Trent? (*Apologising*) I hope I haven't interrupted a *tete a tete*.

TEMPLE: (*Amused*) No, of course not, Charles. Have you had dinner?

MERRITT: Yes, but if there's any of that really excellent coffee, then …

TEMPLE: (*Rather embarrassed*) Oh … er …

STEVE: (*To the rescue*) I'll have a word with Pryce.

STEVE laughs.

MERRITT: M'm … She's rather pretty, isn't she?

TEMPLE: (*Amused*) Yes … Yes, I suppose she is. (*A tiny pause*) Well, any news?

MERRITT: Yes. One of my men went into The Little General yesterday morning and on coming

20

	out he bumped into a fellow known as Skid Tyler.
TEMPLE:	(*Thoughtfully*) Skid Tyler …?
MERRITT:	Yes. D'you know anything about him?
TEMPLE:	Skid Tyler …? Skid … (*Suddenly*) Yes, I know him! He used to be a stunt driver at Brooklands. He was warned off the track in 1930 and served a term in 1931 for share-pushing … or was it '32, I'm not sure which?
MERRITT:	Well, that's the fellow, anyway!
TEMPLE:	(*Thoughtfully*) I wonder what he was doing at The Little General.
MERRITT:	Yes … that's what I wondered. I sent a man back to trail him, but the idiot bungled the job, and Skid disappeared.

The telephone starts to ring.

TEMPLE:	Excuse me. (*He lifts the receiver*) Hello? Paul Temple speaking … Yes … Yes … (*A slight pause*) It's for you, Charles.
MERRITT:	Oh, thanks. (*A pause*) Hello! Who is that? … Oh, hello, Sergeant! … Yes …Yes …Yes … (*Seriously*) Go on … Good Lord! … Yes, yes, of course … You'd better pick me up here … Yes, goodbye.

MERRITT replaces the receiver.

The following dialogue is played tensely and with speed.

TEMPLE:	What is it?
MERRITT:	They've done it again! It's Leamington this time. £14,000 worth of stuff.
TEMPLE:	Phew!
MERRITT:	There'll be hell to pay over this!
TEMPLE:	When did it happen?

MERRITT:	About a quarter of an hour ago. Practically in broad daylight. That smash sounds a dam' funny business to me.
TEMPLE:	What smash?
MERRITT:	A lorry crashed into a dress shop which was next door to the jewellers … There was such a devil of a row over the smash that no one took the slightest notice of what was happening next door.
TEMPLE:	Sounds like a cover to me.
MERRITT:	Yes … that's what I thought.
TEMPLE:	(*Suddenly*) Charles! Tell them to hold that lorry driver!!!
MERRITT:	Why?
TEMPLE:	Because, by Timothy, I bet a fiver it's Skid Tyler!!!!

FADE IN of music.

FADE DOWN music.
FADE IN FORBES speaking.

FORBES:	… It's an interesting story, Miss Trent. Er … very interesting. You say that from the very beginning your brother was under the impression that the brains behind these robberies was this man … er … Max Lorraine … the man who calls himself … the Knave of Diamonds.
STEVE:	Yes, Sir Graham.
FORBES:	M'm. What do you think of all this, Temple?
TEMPLE:	Well, Sir Graham, I don't think there's any doubt that we are up against a man who is, well to say the least of it, out of the ordinary run of criminals. And when we take into

22

	account the fact that Harvey was murdered, surely …
FORBES:	(*Quietly*) What makes you so certain that Harvey was murdered?
TEMPLE:	According to Horace Daley, when Harvey came downstairs he asked him to change a pound note and Daley then went into the back parlour to get the money.
STEVE:	Well?
TEMPLE:	Well, why should he go into the back parlour? There was thirty-seven and sixpence in the till which was on the bar counter.
FORBES:	How do you know all this?
TEMPLE:	Because I examined the till when Daley went upstairs to fetch Miss Parchment down. In fact, that's why I sent him.
FORBES:	M'm.

The door opens.

DALE:	Oh, I'm sorry, sir … I thought you …
FORBES:	Come in, Dale! Come in! You know Paul Temple, I believe?
DALE:	Yes. Yes, of course.
FORBES:	And Miss Trent?
DALE:	How do you do?
STEVE:	How do you do, Inspector?
DALE:	I thought perhaps you'd like to know that Inspector Merritt has arrived, sir … with that man Tyler … Skid Tyler.
FORBES:	Oh, good! Tell Merritt to show him in here … (*Suddenly*) Oh … er … and would you show Miss Trent into Inspector Nelson's office? (*Pleasantly*) We shan't keep you long, Miss Trent.
TEMPLE:	I'll see you later, Steve.

A door closes.

A slight pause.

A second door opens.

FORBES: Sit down, Tyler. No, over there!

SKID: What is it you want? What the 'ell is the idea dragging me along 'ere … anybody would think I was a blarsted criminal.

DALE: Be quiet!

TEMPLE: Yesterday, my dear fellow, with the aid of a two ton lorry, you accidentally smashed your way into a very select little dress shop. By a strange coincidence the shop next door happened to be a jewellers. By an even stranger coincidence it happened to be robbed at precisely the …

SKID: Say, listen, if you're trying to be funny then …

TEMPLE: Trying to be funny? My dear Skid, I'm an amateur humourist compared with the crowd you've been mixing with.

SKID: What … do … you … mean?

TEMPLE: What do I mean? (*Laughing*) Oh! Oh! Our old friend Skid drives the lorry. Our old friend Skid smashes into the dress shop. Our old friend Skid gets arrested. Our old …

SKID: Shut up! Shut yer blasted mouth!!!!

TEMPLE: My dear Skid, don't be a darn fool! Why should you take the rap? Why should you take …

SKID: (*Suddenly*) I'm not talking! I'm not a squealer! I – I know what's good for me!!!!

TEMPLE: (*Determined*) You'll talk to me – and you'll talk fast!!!! What were you doing at Bramley?

24

	What were you doing near The Little General Inn?
SKID:	I tell you, I've never been near the place!!!!
TEMPLE:	Skid, listen … This isn't a one-sided little affair like share-pushing … this is big stuff. This is crime with a capital C. And you're in it! In it up to your neck!!! Now talk …

There is a slight pause.

SKID:	(*Breaking down*) All right … all right … I'll talk. The Inn's used as a sort of … headquarters … We meet there about once a week.
TEMPLE:	Yes, but supposing you don't meet at the Inn?
SKID:	Then we meet at Ashdown House … that's Dr Milton's place … it joins up with the Inn by means of an underground passage …
FORBES:	Dr Milton! Why, that's the doctor who …
TEMPLE:	When is your next meeting?
SKID:	Tomorrow night.
TEMPLE:	At the inn?
SKID:	(*After a pause*) Yes.
TEMPLE:	Skid, the leader of this organisation is a man called Lorraine … Max Lorraine … alias The Knave of Diamonds … that's right, isn't it?
SKID:	Yes … Yes, that's right. (*Suddenly*) Leave me alone! For God's sake, leave me alone!!!! (*He is almost hysterical*)
DALE:	We'd better get him a drink.
FORBES:	Yes. I've got some brandy in that cupboard, Merritt … You might …

The cupboard is opened.

| FORBES: | Ah, thanks! |
| TEMPLE: | (*Gently*) Now, Skid, listen, this is important … have you ever seen this man … Lorraine? |

25

SKID: Leave me alone! For God's sake leave me
               alone!
TEMPLE: Skid, you've got to pull yourself together!
FORBES: Here … drink … this.

A pause.

SKID drinks.

SKID: (*Breathless*) Thanks.
TEMPLE: Now … answer my question, Skid! Have you
               ever seen this man … Mac … (*Suddenly*)
               Skid!!! Skid!!!
FORBES: (*Astonished*) What's the matter?
TEMPLE: Look at him!!!!
DALE: What is it?
MERRITT: (*Suddenly*) Pass me that glass, Sir Graham.
FORBES: The glass …? Good God, man, you don't
               mean …
TEMPLE: (*Quietly*) He's dead …
DALE: Dead!!!!
MERRITT: (*After a pause*) Yes, he's dead, all right.
TEMPLE: What's in the glass, Merritt?
MERRITT: (*Quietly*) Enough cyanide to kill a regiment!
FORBES: But – But that's impossible! Why, it was a
               new bottle, I … I …

The door opens.

LEOPOLD: A lady to see you, sir, by the name of …
FORBES: (*Excitedly*) I can't see anyone! Tell her I'm
               out!
TEMPLE: Oh, just a minute, Sergeant. (*Rather curious*)
               Who … is this lady?
LEOPOLD: It's a Miss Parchment, sir.

FADE IN of music.

FADE DOWN music.

TEMPLE: I'm worried about Miss Trent, Dale. Quite frankly, I don't like the look of things.

DALE: I don't see that's there's anything for you to worry about, sir. You know what these newspaper women are! Here today and …

TEMPLE: (*Irritatedly*) Yes, but I haven't seen or heard anything from her since … (*Suddenly*) Hello, here's Sir Graham!

The door opens.

FORBES: (*Briskly*) Sorry I'm late! I thought Bramley Lodge was the other side of Evesham. (*Surprised*) Oh, hello, Dale! Nothing wrong, I hope?

DALE: No, sir.

FORBES: Are the men all set?

DALE: Yes, sir. I've got Robinson, Black, Jackson, Turner and White watching the Inn, sir. I shall be watching the Doctor's house together with Mowbray, Deal, Hudson and Charters.

FORBES: Good! If anyone attempts to leave, have them picked up. But no-one must be stopped from entering the Inn, you understand?

DALE: Yes, sir.

TEMPLE: And the Doctor's house?

FORBES: At nine-fifteen the men watching the house will close in on it. Force an entrance – and come down the underground passage to the Inn.

TEMPLE: Meanwhile, I suppose the men watching the Inn will follow exactly the same procedure? (*Thoughtfully*) M'm … Well, I should take care of yourself in that passage, Dale. I expect the devils know the place backwards.

DALE: (*Grimly*) Yes.

FORBES: (*Dismissing him*) Well, good luck, Dale. We shall be waiting for you at the Inn.

DALE: Thank you, sir. Good night, Mr Temple ...

TEMPLE: Good night, Inspector ... see you later!

DALE: (*Laughing*) Well, we hope so, sir!

The door closes.

FORBES: I've been on to Fleet Street and I'm rather afraid they ...

TEMPLE: They haven't seen Steve since five o'clock yesterday afternoon. Yes! Yes, I know, Sir Graham! Frankly, I'm worried! Hellishly worried!

FORBES: M'm ... Oh, by the way ... I had that bottle examined ... the one Skid Tyler had the brandy from. It had been tampered with all right.

TEMPLE: Then the poison must have been meant for you, Sir Graham ... and not for Tyler?

FORBES: Yes ... it ... er ... looks very much like it.

TEMPLE: What did Miss Parchment want? Did you see her after ...

FORBES: Yes ... Yes ... It was only a routine call. Actually I sent for Miss Parchment myself. (*Irritated*) She spent the best part of an hour talking about old English Inns ... If you ask me, Temple, I think she's a bit crazy.

TEMPLE laughs.

TEMPLE: What time do you make it?

FORBES: (*Looking at his watch*) It's nearly nine ... Time we were making a move.

TEMPLE: Yes. I'll ring for Pryce ... I'd like a word with him before we leave.

A tiny pause.

FORBES: (*Casually*) Cigarette?

TEMPLE: Oh, thanks.

They light their cigarettes.

PRYCE enters.

PRYCE: You rang, sir?

TEMPLE: Yes. Sir Graham and I are leaving for the Inn,
            Pryce. If Miss Trent should call there's a note
            for her on my writing desk.

PRYCE: Very good, sir.

The door closes.

A slight pause.

TEMPLE: (*Casually*) I say, these cigarettes are rather
            different, aren't they?

FORBES: M'm? Oh, yes … I'm sorry. I ought to have
            told you. I have them specially made for me
            … they're Russian.

TEMPLE: (*Almost indifferent*) Have you always smoked
            them, sir?

FORBES: Oh, yes. (*Almost an afterthought*) Why do
            you ask?

TEMPLE: I wondered … that's all. (*Suddenly*) Ready?

FORBES: Yes, I'm ready …

FADE IN of music.

*FADE DOWN music and CROSS FADE with the sound of a
car.*

*The car stops with a dramatic skid and the grinding of
brakes.*

The car door slams.

FORBES: (*Briskly*) Anything to report, Turner?

TURNER: No, sir.

TEMPLE: Has anyone entered the Inn?

TURNER: Not a soul, sir – I can't understand it.

TEMPLE: (*Quickly*) Come along, Sir Graham.

FORBES: You know the signal, Turner – in case we
            need you.

TURNER: Yes, sir.

A pause.

The door of the Inn is opened.

There is the sound of footsteps.

FORBES: M'm ... place seems deserted.

TEMPLE commences to knock on one of the oak panels.

TEMPLE: There's a gap between here and the staircase
            ... I shouldn't be surprised if there isn't a
            room of ... (*He is sounding the panel*) ...
            some sort.

FORBES: We'd better go upstairs.

TEMPLE: (*Quietly*) Just a minute!

There is a pause.

FORBES: What is it?

TEMPLE: I thought I heard something. (*Suddenly*)
            Listen!

A knock is heard on the wall. The knocking is continued.

FORBES: That's Dale ... he must have come through
            from the house!

TEMPLE: By Timothy, he's been quick!

FORBES: (*Shouting*) Is that you, Dale?

DALE: (*From behind the panel*) Yes!!! Where are
            you?

TEMPLE: It's all right, Sir Graham ... I've found the
            switch ... push the panel back ...

The panel opens.

DALE: (*Rather breathless*) Hello, sir!

FORBES: (*Entering the room*) My God, this place is
            certainly well concealed! Mind your head,
            Temple.

They enter the room.

TEMPLE: Where's the entrance from the house?

DALE:	Through that cupboard, sir … there's another panel. It leads down to the passage.
FORBES:	Well, these people certainly picked a good hide-out. Did you find anyone in the house, Dale?
DALE:	No, sir. (*After a slight hesitation*) But on the small table in the hall I found this.
FORBES:	What is it?
TEMPLE:	It's a playing card – The Knave of Diamonds.
DALE:	There's something on the back, sir.
TEMPLE:	(*Softly*) My God!
FORBES:	What does it say?
TEMPLE:	It says … "Enter Paul Temple … Exit Louise Harvey…"
FORBES:	(*Slowly*) "Exit … Louise Harvey …" (*Suddenly*) Temple! We've got to find that girl!!!!
DALE:	(*Suddenly and rather startled*) Sir Graham!!!
FORBES:	What is it?
DALE:	There's someone in the back parlour. Look, you can see …
TEMPLE:	(*Surprised*) Why, it's Merritt! Hello, Charles!
MERRITT:	Good Lord, Paul! What the devil do you … (*Suddenly amazed*) Sir Graham! Good evening, sir.
FORBES:	Evening, Merritt. What are you doing here?
MERRITT:	I came down to see Mr Temple, sir. His man told me he was down at The Little General and … well, it's lucky you're here too, sir.
FORBES:	Why, what is it, Merritt?
MERRITT:	I'm afraid I've got bad news, sir.
FORBES:	Bad news?
MERRITT:	It's Radcliffe and Chambers of Malvern, sir. They rang through this evening and …

TEMPLE: Radcliffe and Chambers! You mean the jewellers?

MERRITT: Yes.

FORBES: (*Alarmed*) Merritt … you don't mean …?

MERRITT: (*Quietly*) Yes … Nineteen thousand pounds worth.

FORBES: Nineteen thou … Good God, we've certainly fallen for it!

TEMPLE: When did this happen?

MERRITT: About eight o'clock. We've got one of 'em, but I'm afraid they got away with the stuff … (*Suddenly*) Oh, I was forgetting. Pryce asked me to give you this cable, Paul. It arrived about five minutes after you left.

TEMPLE: Oh, thanks! (*He opens the cable*) I've been expecting this. (*After a pause*) You'd better read it, Sir Graham.

FORBES: (*Reading*) "Sydney Bellman was unmarried – but he had a sister …" (*Impatiently*) Who the devil is Bellman?

A knock is heard on one of the back panels.

DALE: (*Surprised*) That's from the cupboard. One of the men must have come through from the house.

FORBES: Open the panel, Dale!

The panel is opened.

DALE: (*Surprised*) Mowbray! What is it? I told you to stay at the house.

MOWBRAY: Sorry, sir. But this lady arrived and insisted on seeing Mr Temple. I thought perhaps …

TEMPLE: (*Surprised*) Miss Parchment!

MISS P: So we meet again, Mr Temple. (*Sweetly*) How nice!

A tiny pause.

FORBES: What – what the devil are you doing here?

TEMPLE: Sir Graham, please! (*Gently*) Miss Parchment
            – I know why you are here tonight – I know
            who you are – and what you are – But there's
            one question you've got to answer. Where is
            Steve Trent?

MISS P: Steve Trent? (*Innocently*) And who, may I
            ask, is Steve Trent?

TEMPLE: Her real name is Harvey – Louise Harvey.
            She's the sister of Superintendent Harvey, the
            man who …

MISS P: (*Alarmed*) Good heavens, you don't mean
            Harvey … had … a sister?

TEMPLE: Yes. And she's disappeared.

MERRITT: (*Surprised*) Disappeared?

TEMPLE: Yes, Charles!

FORBES: You'd better return to the house, Sergeant.

MOWBRAY: Very good, sir.

DALE: I'll come along with you. There's nothing
            further I can do here, Sir Graham.

FORBES: No. Very good, Dale.

The panel closes.

MISS P: Mr Temple, I should very much like to have a
            word with you … er … privately … if
            possible.

TEMPLE: Well …

FORBES: I … er … want to have a chat with Turner, so
            you can come along with me, Merritt.

MERRITT: Very good, sir.

FORBES: Miss Parchment, I shall want to see you later,
            of course.

MISS P: Of course, Sir Graham.

TEMPLE: (*Quietly*) Thank you, Sir Graham.

MERRITT: We'll meet later, Paul.

33

The door opens and closes.

MISS P: (*Quietly*) Who is that man?

TEMPLE: Which man? Oh, Inspector Merritt! Why do you ask?

MISS P: I wondered, that's all. (*Suddenly*) Mr Temple, a little while ago you said: "I know why you are here tonight – I know who you are – and what you are!" (*A slight pause*) Is that true?

TEMPLE: Perfectly.

MISS P: (*After a slight pause*) You don't happen to know, by any chance, why I am interested in old English Inns?

TEMPLE: Yes. Yes, I know, Miss Parchment. (*After a tiny pause*) In Capetown Max Lorraine organised and directed his plans from a group of Inns all situated in the same area. You assumed, quite rightly, that he would adopt the same procedure in this country.

MISS P: (*Thoughtfully*) Yes … (*Suddenly*) Mr Temple, about this girl … Steve Trent …

TEMPLE: Yes?

MISS P: Have you heard of The First Penguin?

TEMPLE: The First Penguin? Why, why, yes. It's a small deserted Inn – on the river. About four miles the other side of Evesham. That's right, isn't it?

MISS P: (*Faintly amused*) That's right, Mr Temple, that's right.

FADE IN of music.

FADE DOWN music.

A telephone is ringing.

DIANA: Hello? … Oh, it's you, Max! … No … No, they haven't … No … Not even Milton. I'm

34

still waiting for them … Yes … Yes, the
girl's here … (*Suddenly*) What? … (*Worried*)
Oh … my God … Yes, I'm listening … Yes
… I'll tell him … Goodbye.

DIANA replaces the receiver.

A door opens.

MILTON: Hello …

DIANA: You're late …

MILTON: (*Almost desperate*) We've had a devil of a
            time over this Malvern business. They've
            picked up Dixie.

DIANA: (*Quietly*) Yes … Yes, I know.

MILTON: What happened about that girl – Steve Trent?

DIANA: She's here.

MILTON: Here?

DIANA: Yes.

MILTON: That's a bit stupid, isn't it?

DIANA: (*After a pause*) I'm glad you came on ahead. I
            wanted to talk to you.

MILTON: Yes, I … er … wanted to see you too.

DIANA: (*Slightly surprised*) Oh?

MILTON: Diana … or shall I say, Ludmilla? … if by
            any chance I happen to have an unfortunate
            … er … accident … either now or in the near
            future, I should like you to know that there is
            a letter … a rather beautifully phrased,
            charmingly written letter, which will be
            delivered straight into the hands of the Home
            Secretary. You will observe that I say the
            Home Secretary – and not Scotland Yard.

DIANA: Max has no intention of double crossing you.
            You've been far too valuable. We respect
            both your intelligence and your courage. But
            …

MILTON: But … what?

DIANA: We've got to get rid of Horace Daley.

A tiny pause.

MILTON: (*Suddenly*) Yes … Yes, all right. Where's the whisky decanter? Oh … Oh, I see …

There is a pause.

DIANA: (*Puzzled*) What's that stuff?

MILTON: (*Amused*) I don't think you'd be any the wiser if I told you, but I feel quite certain that Horace will find it stimulating.

The sound of a car is heard. It is drawing near to the Inn.

DIANA: Here's Horace …

The car stops.

There is a pause.

The door opens.

MILTON: Hello, Horace! You certainly haven't been very long.

HORACE: (*Nervously*) I was stopped again … a rozzer stopped me just outside of Malvern … wanted to see my blasted licence.

DIANA: What happened?

HORACE: Nothin' … but it was ruddy awful while it lasted.

MILTON: (*Laughing*) You need a drink, Horace.

The drink is poured. We hear the sound of a soda syphon.

HORACE: Here … you'd better check the stuff over.

Suddenly a scream is heard from upstairs.

It is obviously STEVE.

She is shouting to be released.

STEVE: (*From somewhere else in the INN*) Let me out of here! Let me out of here, I say!

DIANA: (*Laughing*) You needn't look so jumpy, Horace. There's nothing to be alarmed about.

HORACE: Who is it? Who's upstairs?

MILTON: Steve Trent – she's a reporter on The Evening
            Post.
HORACE: A reporter? Then what the 'ell is she doing
            'ere? You've picked a ruddy good time to
            'ave a reporter hanging about.
MILTON: (*Amused*) Here's your drink …
HORACE: Oh … thanks.
There is a pause.
MILTON: Well … cheerio, Horace …
There is a second pause.
DIANA: What's the matter … are you on the wagon …
            or something?
MILTON: (*Quietly*) Why aren't you drinking, Horace?
HORACE: (*Slowly*) Because I'm not a prize sucker, Doc!
            That's why … (*Taking command*) Now stand
            away from that door … Stand away from that
            door or I'll blow your blasted brains out!
MILTON: Now, listen, Horace. If you take my tip …
HORACE: I'm taking nothing from you, or anybody else,
            from now on, Doc! I'm giving the orders, see!
            Now drink this …
MILTON: (*Alarmed*) No! No!!!!
HORACE: Drink it!!!!
DIANA: (*Calmly*) Here – I'll drink it.
HORACE: (*Slightly surprised*) You …?
DIANA: Yes. There's nothing in the glass except
            whisky … Come … give me the glass, I'll
            prove it.
HORACE: All right! All right, Miss Clever … if that's
            how you feel about it … 'ere we are!
DIANA: Thank you. Well, cheerio, Doc!
Suddenly there is a scuffle.
*It is obvious that DIANA has thrown the contents of the
glass into HORACE's face.*

HORACE: My face! My face! Oh … my face … you …
             you … (*He is almost hysterical with pain*)

*Suddenly, a terrific bang is heard as MILTON strikes him
and HORACE falls to the ground.*

DIANA: Smart work! He's not dead?

MILTON: No, but we'll soon … (*Suddenly*) What's
             that?

*FADE IN the sound of a motor car. It stops, with a sudden
grinding of brakes.*

DIANA: It's a car … (*Surprised*) Why … why it's that
             woman … Miss Parchment!

MILTON: Miss   Parchment!   (*Briskly*)   Open   that
             cupboard door – we'll push Horace in there.

DIANA: Yes, all right.

The cupboard door is opened and HORACE is thrust inside.

DIANA: (*Puzzled*) Doc … who is this woman?

MILTON: Don't ask me … but she seems to be turning
             up all over the place. (*Suddenly*) Here she
             comes – stand away from the door!

A pause.

The door is suddenly thrown open.

MILTON: Good evening, Miss Parchment!!!!

MISS P: Why, Dr Milton! How very nice!

MILTON: (*Briskly*) Come in here! And drop that
             handbag! Drop it!!!

A slight pause.

MISS P: Very well.

MISS PARCHMENT drops her handbag.

MILTON: Pick it up, Diana.

DIANA: O.K.

A pause.

MISS P: I do hope that gun isn't loaded, Doctor. Your
             hand appears to be quite shaky and …

DIANA:	(*Suddenly*) Doc … she's only stalling for time. There's something in the wind, unless I'm very much mistaken …
TEMPLE:	(*Dramatically*) Drop that gun, Milton!!!!
MILTON:	Temple!
DIANA:	How the devil did you get here?
TEMPLE:	I came with Miss Parchment. I regret not having joined you earlier but I had a little difficulty in locating Miss Trent. (*Briskly*) Steve – take his gun!
STEVE:	All right, Paul.
TEMPLE:	Would you mind sitting over there, Miss Thornley …? (*A slight pause*) Thank you. Hold this gun, Miss Parchment – if either of them moves while Miss Trent and I are making them comfortable – well, you know what to do.
MISS P:	Oh … er … rather, Mr Temple!

A slight pause.

STEVE:	Here's the rope, Paul!
TEMPLE:	Thanks. Now for a dose of your own medicine, my friends.

A pause.

MILTON and DIANA are obviously being tied to their chairs.

The telephone commences to ring.

STEVE:	(*Rather excitedly*) Paul … this might be Max Lorraine … Diana was speaking to him earlier in the evening because …
DIANA:	(*Desperately*) That's a lie! That's a lie!
TEMPLE:	(*Quietly*) We'll soon find out.

TEMPLE lifts the receiver.

TEMPLE:	Hello …? Hello …?
STEVE:	What's happened?

TEMPLE: (*After a slight pause*) He's rung off …
STEVE: Did you recognise the voice?
TEMPLE: No. (*Calmly*) But we'll trace the call.

TEMPLE replaces the receiver and then calls the exchange by dialling.

TEMPLE: Hello … Miss … this is Paul Temple speaking … I'm speaking for Sir Graham Forbes, Chief Commissioner of Police … I've just received a telephone call and I want you to trace it for me … Yes … Yes, I know all about that, but this is urgent … desperately urgent … This number is Evesham 9986.
STEVE: (*Anxiously*) Is she tracing it?
TEMPLE: Yes. (*After a tiny pause*) Hello … Yes … (*Surprised*) Are you sure? … I see … Yes … Yes, thank you very much.

TEMPLE replaces the receiver.

MISS P: Well, Mr Temple?
TEMPLE: (*Quietly*) The call came from Bramley Lodge …
STEVE: (*Bewildered*) Bramley Lodge …?
TEMPLE: (*Suddenly making up his mind*) I've got to get back to the house as quickly as possible. If the Knave has been there, and he obviously has, then this is the chance we've been waiting for. Take this revolver, Miss Parchment … if these people try any funny business – use it!
DIANA: (*Angry*) You can't leave us here … tied up like this!
MILTON: Listen, Temple, if you think …
TEMPLE: (*To MISS PARCHMENT*) I'll get Sir Graham to send someone here immediately I get back to the house.

MISS P:	That's all right, Mr Temple. I shall be quite comfortable.
TEMPLE:	Good! We'd better take the Malvern stuff back with us. Give me your handbag, Steve.
STEVE:	Aren't they lovely …
TEMPLE:	(*Briskly*) Now we're all set … See you later, Miss Parchment!
MILTON:	(*Angry*) I'll get you for this, Temple! I'll get you if it takes twenty years!

FADE SCENE.

FADE IN of a motor car ticking over.

TEMPLE:	Jump in!
STEVE:	How long should it take us?
TEMPLE:	About twenty minutes. With a bit of luck we …
STEVE:	(*Puzzled*) Paul … what is it?
TEMPLE:	(*Quietly*) I say, did you see that pigeon?
STEVE:	Why, yes! There's an old courtyard at the back of the Inn, it's full of them. (*Suddenly*) Paul! Paul … I've just thought … they're carrier pigeons!!!!
TEMPLE:	Yes, they're carrier pigeons all right! (*Suddenly*) Well … and now for Bramley Lodge. (*Softly*) And the Knave of Diamonds!!!!

FADE IN of the car making a speedy departure.
The noise of the car is held for a little while.

MILTON:	(*Angry*) Miss Parchment … if you don't release both …
MISS P:	My dear Dr Milton, if I've told you once, I've told you a hundred times, there is absolutely nothing to be gained by these … er …

41

	primitive outbursts. You're staying in that chair until Mr Temple returns, and if there's any … er … funny business I shall press this trigger … I shall press this trigger, Dr Milton!
MILTON:	When I get out of this I'll …
DIANA:	Shut up, Doc!!! Shut up!!! (*Quietly*) There's nothing to be gained by kicking up a row. We're in a jam and we've got to make the best of it.
MISS P:	Ah, you have a philosophical side to your nature, Miss … Thornley. I congratulate you!!!

Suddenly in the background a noise is heard.

It is obviously HORACE in the cupboard having 'come round' after his encounter with MILTON and DIANA.

MISS P:	(*Suddenly*) What's that?
MILTON:	(*Quickly to DIANA*) It's Horace!
DIANA:	If we can get him to …

The door of the cupboard opens and simultaneously DIANA cries out.

| DIANA: | Look out, Horace!!! Look out!!! |

There is a revolver shot.

| MILTON: | (*Excitedly*) She's missed him!!! |

There is a brief struggle as HORACE relieves MISS PARCHMENT of the revolver.

HORACE:	Oh, no you don't, Miss Parchment … or whatever your name is …
DIANA:	Good, Horace!!!! Good!!!!
HORACE:	I don't know what the 'ell you're doing 'ere but get in that cupboard! Get in that cupboard!
MISS P:	Mr Daley, I must ask you to …

There is the sound of a struggle … heavy breathing etc.

| HORACE: | Get in that cupboard or by God I'll … |

The cupboard door closes with a bang.

MILTON: Get us untied, Horace – quickly!!!

HORACE: (*Still obviously in a daze through being struck on the head by MILTON*) Strewth, my 'ead! It's like a blasted furnace …

DIANA: Horace! Untie us – quickly …

HORACE: What? Oh, no you don't … (*Suddenly*) 'Ello, where's the Malvern stuff?

MILTON: Horace, for God's sake don't stand there … get this rope untied … We must get out of here …

DIANA: Quickly, Horace!!!

HORACE: (*Angry*) Listen, you two … where's the stuff?

MILTON: Get the rope free, Horace, and then …

HORACE: (*Desperately*) Now listen, Doc … if you don't tell me where the stuff is I'll break every single bone in …

MILTON: N … No!!! No!!! (*Quickly*) All right … all right … (*A tiny pause*) Temple's got it. He left about ten minutes ago with the girl …

HORACE: That's all I want to know!!!

The door bangs.

DIANA: (*Shouting*) Horace … Horace …

MILTON: The dirty, double crossing, little swine … When I get … (*He is struggling*) … out of here I'll …

MISS PARCHMENT commences to bang on the cupboard door.

MISS P: (*Shouting from inside the cupboard*) Let me out of here! Let me out of here! Let me out of here, I say!!!

FADE VOICES completely.

FADE IN of music.

43

FADE MUSIC slowly.

FADE IN of a car cruising at a fairly fast speed.

STEVE: How far have we got to go now, Paul?

TEMPLE: Not very far … about a mile. (*After a pause*) Thank God Miss Parchment knew about The First Penguin.

STEVE: (*Puzzled*) Paul … who is Miss Parchment?

TEMPLE: Her name is Bellman. Amelia Bellman … she's the sister of the detective who helped your brother over the Capetown-Simonstown … (*Suddenly*) I say, look at this car behind … it seems to be travelling rather …

STEVE: (*Alarmed*) Paul! It's Daley … Horace Daley!!!!

TEMPLE: Daley!!!!

STEVE: He's recognised us!! (*Frightened*) Paul, he's got a gun, he's … Look out, Paul! Look out!!!!

A revolver shot is heard above the roar of the car – followed by the smashing of glass.

TEMPLE: Steve! Are you all right?

STEVE: Yes … He hit the window at the back …

TEMPLE: Keep down!!!!

STEVE: Paul … He's going to pass you …

TEMPLE: No … No, we mustn't let him do that …

TEMPLE's car shoots forward.

TEMPLE: (*Suddenly*) Steve, listen … there's a bridge round the next bend … As soon as we reach it I'll slow down and let him overtake us … Then we'll force him over the top … It's our only chance …

STEVE: Yes … Yes, all right!!!!

TEMPLE: Wrap the rug round your head and keep down …

STEVE: Look out!!!!

Another revolver shot is heard – followed by the smashing of glass.

TEMPLE: It's only the windscreen!!! Keep down!!!!

STEVE: Paul … you're hurt!

TEMPLE: No … No, I'm all right …

The cars turn the corner at a terrific speed ...

There is a slight pause.

TEMPLE: Here's the bridge. Now keep down!!!!

STEVE: He's passing us, Paul! Look out, he's forcing you over … He's …

TEMPLE: Hold on, Steve!!!!

A tremendous crash is heard as TEMPLE forces HORACE's car into the bridge ...

This is followed by a second crash, and an enormous splash, as part of the stone bridge gives way under the impact and HORACE's car pitches into the river …

TEMPLE: Steve!!!! Are you all right?

STEVE: (*A little breathless*) Yes … Yes … I'm … all … right … (*Alarmed*) Paul!!! You're hurt!

TEMPLE: No … No … It's nothing … It's only a scratch … (*Suddenly*) I say, we'd better get out of here … the car's half over the bridge … Careful …

TEMPLE and STEVE climb out of the car.

STEVE: (*Alarmed*) Paul! Look! There's Horace … He's on the side … He must have been thrown out of the car … against the wall.

TEMPLE: (*Very seriously*) Yes … yes … he's in a pretty bad way … Wait here, Steve …

A pause.

Temple walks across the bridge.

FADE IN of HORACE groaning in a very low voice. He is obviously dying.

45

TEMPLE: (*Gently*) Horace … listen … Who is … the …
             Knave? (*A pause*) Horace! (*Softly*) Horace!
A pause.
STEVE arrives.
STEVE: How … is he?
TEMPLE: (*Slowly*) He's … dead. (*A pause*) We'll have
             to walk to Bramley Lodge, Steve. It's about
             half a mile … I think.
FADE IN of music.

FADE DOWN music.
A motor car is ticking over rather quietly.
PRYCE: (*Calling in a whisper*) Miss Trent! Miss
             Trent!!!
STEVE: Oh, here you are, Pryce!
PRYCE: (*Confidentially*) I've brought the small car
             down, miss. Mr Temple said you would take
             over from … (*Suddenly*) Oh, here <u>is</u> Mr
             Temple!
TEMPLE: (*Slightly breathless*) Sorry to have kept you
             waiting at the gate, Steve. Oh … You've got
             the car … Good! Now get back to the house,
             Pryce … and remember what I said … not a
             word to a soul … except for that message I
             gave you.
PRYCE: Yes, sir. Goodnight, sir. Goodnight, miss.
PRYCE departs.
STEVE: (*Puzzled*) Paul … what have you been doing
             up at the house?
TEMPLE: I wrote a letter …
STEVE: Is that all?
TEMPLE: Yes.
STEVE: Didn't you see anyone?

TEMPLE: No. (*Slowly*) Merritt, Dale, and Sir Graham
            are in the drawing room … but I didn't see
            them.

STEVE: (*Puzzled*) But why not?

TEMPLE: Steve … listen …I'm going across the tennis
            court to the front of the drawing-room. They
            won't be able to see me from there … I shall
            be gone about two minutes … Keep the car
            running.

STEVE: But – But what are you going to do?

TEMPLE: I can't explain now, Steve. But as soon as I
            get back to the car … let it rip!

STEVE: Yes. Yes, all right!!!!

FADE IN the car ticking over.
SLOW FADE.

FADE IN of voices. We are in the drawing room with SIR
GRAHAM, INSPECTOR DALE and INSPECTOR
MERRITT.

FORBES: (*Irritated*) Well, I'm dashed if I can
            understand it! We must have been here nearly
            two hours!

DALE: Did Temple say he was coming back here,
            sir?

FORBES: Yes, of course he did, Dale. After the raid on
            the Inn he left with Miss Parchment and said
            he'd meet us here at Bramley Lodge, didn't
            he, Merritt?

MERRITT: That's right, sir.

DALE: Well, he wasn't at the doctor's house.
            Certainly not when I left.

FORBES: Of course he wasn't! What the devil would he
            be …

Suddenly a noise of broken glass is heard.

It is obvious that a stone has been pitched through the French windows.

DALE: What the devil is that?

FORBES: It's a stone!!!

MERRITT: Yes … it came through the French windows … Look!

DALE: A stone …? But why on earth should anyone … I say, look … there's a piece of paper wrapped round it …

MERRITT: Yes … Yes … It's a note!

DALE: What is it, Sir Graham?

FORBES: Just a second … (*He picks up the note and straightens it out*) Ah, here we are …

A slight pause.

DALE: Well?

A tiny pause.

MERRITT: What is it?

FORBES: (*Slowly*) It says: "Temple caught … First Penguin awaiting instructions … Malvern pigeons despatched … Ludmilla …"

MERRITT: Temple … caught!!!!

DALE: (*Puzzled*) Ludmilla … Who the devil is Ludmilla?

FORBES: This business seems to get more complicated week after week.

DALE: (*Thoughtfully*) Malvern pigeons despatched … (*Suddenly*) Why … that must have something to do with the robbery at Malvern … Surely, that's why …

MERRITT: (*Quietly*) Good God!

FORBES: What is it?

MERRITT: We are damn fools! Don't you see … that's how they've been getting some of the small stuff out of the country.

48

DALE: You mean ... by pigeons ... carrier pigeons
           ...?
MERRITT: Yes.
FORBES: (*Astonished*) Well, I'm damned!!!!
A slight pause.
FORBES: Well, I'm damned!
MERRITT: But, Sir Graham, why should they give the
           game away, in a note like this ... "Malvern
           pigeons despatched" ... They must have
           known we'd guess.
FORBES: They're not worried about our guessing their
           little secrets now, Merritt. All they're
           concerned about is getting the whole matter
           straightened out, and then vanishing. And, by
           Gad, it looks as if they're doing it ... They've
           got Temple ... and they've got the girl.
DALE: Yes, but that still doesn't explain why this
           note was thrown through the window, Sir
           Graham. The note was obviously meant for
           the Knave of Diamonds.
MERRITT: That's right.
DALE: Then this girl – er –
FORBES: Ludmilla.
DALE: ... Ludmilla, must believe that the Knave is
           here. Here, in this house.
FORBES: But there isn't anyone here except us and –
DALE: (*Interrupting*) And Pryce.
FORBES: Yes, and Pryce.
MERRITT: Oh, but Pryce is out of the question, why – it
           can't possibly be him ... can it?
DALE: The thing that really beats me is this First
           Penguin reference. What the devil, or who the
           devil, is the First Penguin?
MERRITT: That's what I'd like to know.

DALE:	Can you think what they mean, sir?
FORBES:	I'm damned if I can! I say, I hope Steve Trent and Temple are all right: if anything happens to them …
MERRITT:	Yes. Yes, I hope so too.
FORBES:	Well, look here, it's no good staying here all night. I'm getting back to the Yard with the note. I'd like Henderson to have a look at it. He can make sense out of any damn thing.
DALE:	I'll pick Turner up at The Little General, then Mowbray and company at Ashdown House. Is that all right, Sir Graham?
FORBES:	Yes. I should bring Turner back here and let him keep a guard on the house. He might keep an eye on this feller – er – Pryce.
DALE:	Yes, Sir Graham.

FADE IN of music.

FADE DOWN of music.

DIANA:	If I could only get this rope free at the back I could … could … move my arms and then … then …
MILTON:	When I get my hands on that little swine Horace … I'll …
DIANA:	(*Thoughtfully*) I hope Horace caught Temple before he got to Bramley Lodge …
MILTON:	I wonder what on earth made Max ring up from Temple's place. That was a damn fool thing to do, if you like.
DIANA:	(*Irritated*) Why was it? How was he to know that Temple would … (*Suddenly*) Hello …? What's that?

FADE IN of a car drawing up to the Inn.

MILTON:	It's a car!!!!

DIANA: Yes … I hope to God it's Max …

A pause.

Footsteps are heard.

The door opens.

MILTON: (*Surprised*) Temple!

TEMPLE: Yes, my dear Milton – You must forgive me for once again …

STEVE: (*Suddenly surprised*) Paul … Where's Miss Parchment?

TEMPLE: Yes!!! Yes, where is she, Milton? (*A pause*) Milton, if you don't …

DIANA: She's gone! She left about an hour ago …

TEMPLE: (*Quickly*) Why …? Why did she leave …?

A pause.

MILTON and DIANA refuse to answer.

TEMPLE: Well, perhaps it's a good job you don't feel like talking!

MILTON: (*Slightly alarmed*) What … What are you going to do …?

TEMPLE: Just … er … gag you, my friend … We don't want you to be unnecessarily noisy, when our distinguished guest arrives. (*Briskly*) Here – you attend to the girl, Steve …

DIANA: Distinguished guest …?

TEMPLE: A friend of yours, Miss Thornley. A very close friend, if I'm not mistaken.

DIANA: (*Alarmed*) Not … Not … Max! (*Suddenly desperate*) No!!!! No!!!! (*She continues to shout, but STEVE has already gagged her … and after a series of muffled exclamations … there is silence*)

TEMPLE: Now … turn the light out, Steve!

The light is turned out.

TEMPLE: Good … and now … we … wait!

51

A pause.

STEVE: (*Quietly excited*) Paul ... is ... is he really coming here?

TEMPLE: Yes. Yes, I think so, Steve.

STEVE: You're not certain?

TEMPLE: One can never be too certain of people ... Least of all, people like Max Lorraine ...

STEVE: But, Paul ... Why should he come here? For what ...

TEMPLE: (*Quietly*) Because I've laid a trap, Steve ... A rather neat little trap with ... (*He hesitates*)

STEVE: What is it?

A pause.

TEMPLE: Listen!

FADE IN of a car drawing up to the Inn.

STEVE: (*Excited and amazed*) Paul ... Paul ... he's here ...

TEMPLE: (*Softly*) By Timothy ... yes! (*Briskly*) Steve ... stand by the light ... When I give the signal, switch it on.

STEVE: (*Excitedly*) Yes ... Yes, all right.

TEMPLE: Sh! Quiet, Steve!

A long pause.

Footsteps are heard.

The door opens.

VOICE: Ludmilla! Ludmilla!!! (*Alarmed*) Ludmilla, where are you? Why don't you ... (*Suspiciously*) Who's there?!!!

TEMPLE: (*Briskly*) Lights, Steve!!!

The lights are switched on.

TEMPLE: Drop that gun!!!

VOICE: Temple!

STEVE: (*Amazed*) Why ... Why, it's Dale ... Inspector Dale!!!

TEMPLE:	… Yes, Inspector Dale … alias Max Lorraine, alias The Knave of Diamonds!!!!
DALE:	Temple, are you mad!!! What the devil does this mean?
TEMPLE:	Briefly, my dear Lorraine – it means … Exit The Knave! (*Briskly*) Steve – ungag the girl …
DALE:	(*Furious – yet puzzled*) Ludmilla … Why did you send that note …?
DIANA:	(*Amazed*) Note …? What note …?
DALE:	Good God, you don't mean … Temple!!!
TEMPLE:	Yes, I sent the note … My method of delivering it was a little unconventional, I admit … But it seems to have served its purpose …
DIANA:	You damn fool, Max … you've played straight into his hands, why …

The door opens.

SERGEANT MORRISON, INSPECTOR MERRITT, SIR GRAHAM FORBES and CONSTABLE MILLER arrive.

TEMPLE:	Ah, hello, Sir Graham! Hello, Charles!
FORBES:	(*Slowly*) So you've got Milton … and Dale.
TEMPLE:	Yes.
FORBES:	I don't mind telling you, Temple, that I was pretty well bowled over when Pryce gave me your message.
TEMPLE:	Yes, I expect you were, Sir Graham.
MERRITT:	Have you searched him?
TEMPLE:	Not yet, Charles.
MERRITT:	Right. We'll wait till we get him back to the station.
FORBES:	Take Milton and the girl to the car, Sergeant.
MORRISON:	Yes, sir. Come along, Miller, give me a hand. You untie the girl.

53

A slight pause.

MILTON: (*Now free – with a sigh of relief*) Well, they say – give a man plenty of rope and he'll hang himself … And you've certainly made a pretty good job of it, Max.

MORRISON: Come along, you!

MILTON: Goodbye, Mr Temple. This time, I'm afraid … we shan't meet again.

MORRISON: Bring the girl too, Miller.

MILLER: Yes, sir.

A slight pause.

DIANA: So – So … it's goodbye, Max.

DALE: Yes. Yes, it's goodbye. (*Quietly*) But … remember what I always said, Ludmilla … They won't take me … They won't take me …

MORRISON: Come along, miss.

The door closes.

DALE: Do you mind if I have a cigarette, Sir Graham?

FORBES: (*Hesitatingly*) No – all right. (*A slight pause*) You can have one of mine.

DALE: If you don't mind, I'd rather not. I don't particularly care for your brand of Russian cigarettes. I have my own. (*Calmly*) Have you a light, Merritt?

A pause.

FORBES: (*Quietly*) It's all right, Merritt.

DALE: (*Blowing a cloud of smoke*) Ah, thank you – that's better.

MERRITT: (*With authority*) I think we'll have the bracelets on, sir. Just to be on the safe side.

The handcuffs are slipped on DALE.

DALE: Well … I've had a good run for my money … and I'm not grumbling … it's a pity you caught me on a cheap trick, Temple, but – I guess that's how things turn out sometimes …

FORBES: Dale … tell me … that time when Skid Tyler was poisoned. What happened?

DALE: (*Amused – laughing slightly*) The poison wasn't meant for Tyler. I can assure you of that, Sir Graham …

FORBES: Then … Then it must have been meant for me!

DALE continues to laugh … a rather long, mirthless laugh. Suddenly the laughter stops and he starts to cough – he is obviously a little dizzy and unsteady on his feet.

FORBES: What the devil is it, Dale?

STEVE: (*Alarmed*) Paul, he's going to faint.

TEMPLE: (*Quickly*) My God – it's the cigarette. He's poisoned himself.

DALE: (*Weakly but rather boastfully*) I told Ludmilla you'd never take me.

DALE starts to laugh again but rather weakly.

TEMPLE: (*Quickly*) Get him to the car, Merritt! Get him to the car!

FORBES: We'll have to get him into Evesham.

DALE falls to the ground.

MERRITT: He's spark out. We'll have to be quick, Sir Graham.

FORBES: Here. I'll … that's right, Merritt. Careful!

The door closes.

A pause.

STEVE: (*Puzzled*) Paul … why did the Knave come here? Did you know it was Dale? And why …

TEMPLE: (*Amused*) One question at a time, Steve! (*Seriously*) I'd had my suspicions about Dale

	for quite a little while, and when I got back to Bramley Lodge and found that …
STEVE:	But he wasn't the only person at Bramley Lodge.
TEMPLE:	(*Quietly*) No. There was Sir Graham and Merritt. Sir Graham of course was really quite out of the question … although even with Sir Graham I found myself occasionally … well … wondering … I think it was those Russian cigarettes he smoked.
STEVE:	But there was Merritt.
TEMPLE:	(*Thoughtfully*) Yes – there was Merritt. And quite frankly he rather worried me. You see, Merritt was in Sir Graham's office the day Skid Tyler was murdered. Merritt knew that you were Louise Harvey … and he turned up tonight at The Little General when the Inn was raided.
STEVE:	Yes. But I still don't see how you managed to trick Dale into …
TEMPLE:	I'm coming to that, Steve … When I got back to the house and discovered that Sir Graham, Merritt and Dale were in the drawing room – I decided to find out, once and for all, who was the Knave! I scribbled a short note which said: "Temple caught … First Penguin awaiting instructions … Malvern pigeons despatched … Ludmilla." … This I pitched through the drawing room window. Now the note would, I felt sure, read like utter nonsense to everyone in that room, except of course … Max Lorraine. And Lorraine would, I felt confident, immediately assume that Temple had been caught and that Milton and

Ludmilla, alias Diana Thornley, were waiting for him at The First Penguin.

STEVE: Yes. Yes, I see.

TEMPLE: The phrase – "First Penguin awaiting instructions" would of course sound like the most utter balderdash to Sir Graham and Merritt, who wouldn't even know what The First Penguin stood for. Dale knew perfectly well what the note meant, however, and acted accordingly. So now you know …

The door opens.

TEMPLE: (*Surprised*) Hello, Charles! What is it?

MERRITT: (*Slowly*) He's – He's dead, Paul.

STEVE: (*Softly*) Dead!

A pause.

TEMPLE: I – I see.

A slight pause.

MERRITT: I thought perhaps you'd like to know.

TEMPLE: (*Quickly*) Yes – Yes, of course. Thank you, Charles.

MERRITT: (*With a sigh of relief*) Well, personally, I can't say I'm sorry this business is over. It certainly put the wind up me.

TEMPLE: (*Slightly puzzled*) Why do you say that?

MERRITT: Well, as a matter of fact, Paul … I've literally been quivering in my shoes since the very first day I heard about The Knave of Diamonds.

TEMPLE: But – why?

MERRITT: When I was a small and rather energetic youngster of about nine, I fell off a tricycle, Paul. It made a scar. A rather small scar above the right elbow.

TEMPLE: (*Greatly amused*) Oh – Oh, I see.

57

Both STEVE and TEMPLE laugh.

MERRITT: (*Pleasantly*) I'll see you both later at Bramley Lodge.

The door closes.

STEVE: (*With a sigh*) Well – this brings us to the end of our little adventure.

TEMPLE: Yes, I'm afraid it does. (*Quietly*) Exit, The Knave!

A pause.

STEVE: I want to get back to Town as quickly as possible. This story is rather important and the paper always …

TEMPLE: (*Suddenly*) Steve!!!!

STEVE: Yes?

TEMPLE: I was wondering if you … er …

STEVE: Well?

TEMPLE: If you'd … er … care to have dinner with me on … on Thursday?

STEVE: Thursday? Yes, of course … I'd love to.

TEMPLE: Good. I shall be in Town … so perhaps we can … we … lunch together, too …?

STEVE: Yes, why not?

TEMPLE: We might even manage to have tea together as a sort of … er … sort of … er …

STEVE: (*Quietly*) I'd love to.

TEMPLE: Oh … er … splendid. Well, that's about all … (*Quickly*) Of course, there is breakfast but …

STEVE: (*Calmly*) I always have breakfast in bed.

TEMPLE: In bed?

STEVE: Yes.

TEMPLE: Oh … er … well, that's a bit awkward.

STEVE: Of course … we could get married.

TEMPLE: Yes, I suppose we … (*Suddenly amazed*) I say … I say … are you proposing?

STEVE: (*Imitating TEMPLE*) What do you think, Mr Temple? What do you think?

TEMPLE: (*Laughing*) Well, of all the unconventional little devils you simply …

Suddenly in the background a terrific bang is heard, followed by several more.

STEVE: (*Alarmed*) What's that?

TEMPLE: (*Seriously*) It's from the cupboard!!!!

STEVE: Yes. Yes, what is it?

TEMPLE: (*Dramatically*) We'll soon find out. Stand on one side, Steve!!! Stand on one side!!!

The door of the cupboard bursts open.

TEMPLE: Why – Why, it's Miss Parchment!!!!

STEVE: Miss Parchment!!!!

MISS P: (*Exhausted*) For heaven's sake, give me some air!!!! Oh, dear … Oh, dear … (*Suddenly*) Hello, where's Dr Milton and … the girl?

TEMPLE: (*Seriously*) They've gone, Miss Parchment …

MISS P: Gone!

TEMPLE: They've been arrested. (*A slight pause*) And the Knave's gone too … He's dead … It was Dale … Inspector Dale of Scotland Yard.

MISS P: (*Completely amazed*) You – You mean to say … all this has been going on while I've been in that … blasted cupboard?

TEMPLE: Yes.

MISS P: (*Staggered*) Well … By Timothy!!!!

FADE IN of closing music.

THE END

NEWS OF
PAUL TEMPLE

An abridged version of the radio serial
presented as a complete play
By FRANCIS DURBRIDGE
Broadcast on BBC Radio
5 July 1944
CAST:

Paul Temple . . . . .Richard Williams

Steve, his wife . . . . .Lucille Lisle

Sir Graham Forbes . . . . . . .Laidman Browne

Mrs Weston . . . . Gladys Young

Ernie Weston . . . . .Preston Lockwood

Iris Archer . . . . .Grizelda Hervey

Rex Bryant . . . . .Lewis Stringer

Mrs Moffat . . . . Molly Rankin

Laurence Van Draper . . . . . Alexander Sarner

Major Guest . . . . .Cyril Gardiner

David Lindsay . . . . .Basil Jones

Ben Collins . . . . Frank Cochrane

An Editor . . . . Arthur Ridley

Alec . . . . Duncan McIntyre

OPEN TO:

ANNOUNCER: Thirty-second Street anchorage on the East River! The Golden Clipper, first flying boat of new Anglo-American air combine, leaves for Southampton. Beginning of fifteen-hour trans-Atlantic air service. Southampton in fifteen hours!!!

FADE IN of The Golden Clipper …
It is obviously travelling at a tremendous speed.
The sound of the engine is deep and heavy.
FADE DOWN slowly.
The FADE gives the impression of the plane passing into the distance.

FADE IN of a typewriter.
The sound of voices, in the background a news machine is ticking away.

EDITOR: (*Excited*) Where's Bryant? Where the devil is Bryant? My God, what a life! Bryant! Bryant!!!

REX: (*Playfully, singing the words*) Do I hear you calling me?

EDITOR: You should have been here hours ago! Get down to Southampton! Cover the Golden Clipper story!

REX: Don't make me laugh! That isn't a story … New York to Southampton in fifteen hours!

EDITOR: (*With heavy sarcasm*) I don't suppose you know by any chance who happens to be travelling on The Clipper?

REX: The Quintuplets?

EDITOR: Not exactly! Just … Paul Temple!

REX: (*Surprised*) Paul Temple?

EDITOR: Mr and Mrs Paul Temple to be more precise
              …

REX: Are you sure?

EDITOR: Of course I'm sure!

REX: I expect he's coming over for the rehearsals
              of his new play.

EDITOR: Don't you ever read the papers? The play's
              off – the leading lady's walked out! She's
              gone to South America!

REX: Walked out! You mean … Iris Archer?

EDITOR: Yes, Iris Archer! Get down to Southampton
              and see what Temple's got to say about it.

REX: I'd sooner cover that new movie at The
              Empire.

EDITOR: Southampton! You son of a … foreign
              correspondent.

REX: Okay. Snow White! O.K.!!!

FADE IN of music.

FADE DOWN music.

FADE IN of background noises of the airport.

There is a background of voices.

REX: Come on, Temple, let's have the true story
              about Iris Archer! What made her change her
              mind about the play?

TEMPLE: I haven't the vaguest idea!

REX: I thought she was crazy about it.

TEMPLE: So did I! All I know is that shortly before we
              left New York I received this cable – read it
              yourself!

REX: (*Reading*) "Terribly sorry compelled to cancel
              play. Stop. Leaving for South America. Stop.
              Will write later. Stop. Lots of love …"

TEMPLE:	Stop!
REX:	M'm … Well, what are your plans for the future?
STEVE:	We haven't got any plans, have we, darling?
TEMPLE:	No.
REX:	(*Irritatedly*) Look here, Temple, I've got to take some kind of story back to Town with me! Have you been in touch with Scotland Yard recently? Have you heard anything from Sir Graham Forbes while you've …
STEVE:	No, we haven't heard anything from Sir Graham! And we don't want to hear anything either!

TEMPLE laughs.

STEVE:	Sir Graham's a darling, but he makes life altogether too hectic!
REX:	(*Faintly exasperated*) Well, what are you going to do?
STEVE:	(*Sweetly*) We're going to Scotland, Rex … for three weeks … on a holiday.
REX:	(*Contemptuously*) Scotland?
STEVE:	Yes.
REX:	For three weeks!???
TEMPLE:	Yes.
REX:	On a holiday?!!
TEMPLE:	Yes.
REX:	(*Finally exasperated*) Well, I hope it keeps fine for you!!!

FADE IN of music.

FADE DOWN music.
FADE in of a motor car.
Coupled with the noise of the car is the sound of heavy thunder and torrential rain.

STEVE:	(*Alarmed*) Oh, Paul!
TEMPLE:	It's all right, darling!
STEVE:	The storm seems to be getting worse.
TEMPLE:	I wish this confounded windscreen would keep … (*His voice fades in yet another roll of thunder*)
STEVE:	I wonder how many miles we are from Inverdale?
TEMPLE:	I'm beginning to wonder whether there is such a place! (*A slight pause*) This looks like a village.

The car slows down.

TEMPLE:	It's no good going on if we're not on the right road.
STEVE:	Well, stop the car and I'll get the map out.

The car pulls up.

TEMPLE:	(*Quietly*) I say, that second cottage is some sort of a shop by the look of things. They'd put us on the right track.
STEVE:	Yes, perhaps it would be quicker.
TEMPLE:	I shan't be a second, darling!

TEMPLE gets out of the car and slams the door.

FADE the car into the background.

TEMPLE arrives at the cottage.

The door of the shop opens, there is a sudden clanging of a distant bell.

The door closes.

MRS MOFFAT arrives. She is a tight-lipped Scotswoman with a monotonous, almost mechanical voice.

MRS MOFFAT:	Good evening!
TEMPLE:	Oh, good evening!
MRS MOFFAT:	What can I get ye?
TEMPLE:	Well – er – I should like some chocolate.

MRS MOFFAT:	We don't keep chocolate.
TEMPLE:	Oh, I see. Then I'll take some postcards.
MRS MOFFAT:	A packet?
TEMPLE:	Yes … a packet.
MRS MOFFAT:	Six delightful views of Inverdale – two by moonlight. That'll be sixpence.
TEMPLE:	(*Pleasantly*) That's all right.
MRS MOFFAT:	I'll put them in an envelope for ye …

A slight pause.

TEMPLE:	Thank you. How far is Inverdale from here?
MRS MOFFAT:	About two miles. (*After a moment*) You're a stranger round these parts …?
TEMPLE:	Very much so, I'm afraid.
MRS MOFFAT:	Have ye come far?
TEMPLE:	(*Quietly*) London.
MRS MOFFAT:	(*Almost pleasantly*) London? That's a long way …
TEMPLE:	Yes.
MRS MOFFAT:	I've a married sister in London. Peckham, I believe. Is there a place called Peckham?
TEMPLE:	Yes. There is a place called Peckham.
MRS MOFFAT:	(*With a sigh*) It must be a wonderful thing to travel. I often wish I had the time … an' the money of course. What was it Shakespeare said about travellers …?
TEMPLE:	He said so many things.
MRS MOFFAT:	(*Coldly, almost as if she had never started a conversation*) Here's ye change.
TEMPLE:	Thanks.

The door suddenly opens.

There is a sudden clanging of the bell.
DAVID LINDSAY arrives.
He is a very excitable young man of about twenty-eight.
Just at the moment he is out of breath.

MRS MOFFAT: (*Surprised*) Why, Mr Lindsay!

LINDSAY: Hel ... Hello, Mrs Moffat!

MRS MOFFAT: Goodness me, you have been running!

LINDSAY: I'm sorry ... bursting in ... like this, but ... but ... (*To TEMPLE*) No, don't go, sir! (*After a slight pause*) I saw your car about a quarter of a mile back. Then when I saw you stop at Mrs Moffat's I ... I raced along here. I was afraid that you might get started again before ... before I could get here in time.

TEMPLE: In time? What is it you want?

LINDSAY: I was wondering if you happened to be going to Inverdale?

TEMPLE: Yes. Yes, as a matter of fact, I am.

LINDSAY: Then ... would you be good enough to do me a favour?

TEMPLE: Well, I might. What is it exactly?

LINDSAY: There's an inn at Inverdale called The Royal Gate. I don't know whether you know it or not?

TEMPLE: As a matter of fact my wife and I intend staying the night at Inverdale so ...

LINDSAY: Oh, that's splendid! Well, when you get to the inn would you be good enough to ask for a Mr John Richmond, and then ... (*His voices falters slightly*) give him this letter.

LINDSAY hands TEMPLE a letter.

TEMPLE: Mr John Richmond … (*Suddenly*) Why, yes, I'll do that with pleasure.

LINDSAY: (*Earnestly*) Please realise that this is most important. Under no circumstances must you give the letter to anyone else … under no circumstances …

TEMPLE: But supposing this Mr Richmond doesn't happen to be staying at the inn?

LINDSAY: (*Quietly*) He'll be there all right.

TEMPLE: (*Suddenly*) Well, don't worry about the letter – I'll see your friend gets it. (*After a tiny pause*) It's a straight road into the village, I gather …?

LINDSAY: Perfectly. You can't possibly go wrong. The Royal Gate is on the left-hand side, about half-way through …

TEMPLE: Thanks. Goodnight.

MRS MOFFAT: (*Quietly*) You're forgetting your postcards.

TEMPLE: Oh, yes, of course! Goodnight!

The door opens and closes.
FADE SCENE.

FADE up of the motor car.
A pause.

STEVE: I don't know what you think, darling, but this seems to me to be an awfully long two miles!

TEMPLE: It does rather …

A pause.

STEVE: He appeared to be in an awful hurry, didn't he?

TEMPLE: (*Quietly*) You mean the young man who gave me the letter?

69

STEVE: Yes. He came dashing down the road as if
                his very life depended on it. I thought
                there'd been an accident.

The sound of a second car is heard.
It is approaching very quickly.

STEVE: There's a car behind, darling … He wants
                to pass you.

The sound of the second car is much louder.
He is obviously overtaking.

TEMPLE: By Timothy, this fellow seems to …

STEVE: (*Rather excitedly*) He wants you to stop,
                darling!

TEMPLE: Stop?

STEVE: He's pulling up … You'll have to stop,
                Paul!

With a sudden grinding of brakes, both cars are finally at a
standstill.

TEMPLE: I bet a fiver the poor devil's lost.

STEVE: There's two of them.

TEMPLE: I like the way they've parked their car … I
                couldn't get past if I wanted to!

The sound of footsteps.
LAURENCE VAN DRAPER and MAJOR GUEST arrive.
VAN DRAPER is a man of about thirty-eight.
MAJOR GUEST is about fifty-five.
Both are well spoken.
VAN DRAPER's voice, however, is a little too suave to be
sincere.

VAN DRAPER: Really, sir, I must apologise for stopping
                you like this, but unfortunately we …

STEVE: (*Brightly*) If it's the road to Inverdale you
                want then …

VAN DRAPER: Unfortunately, madam, it is not the road to
                Inverdale we want.

GUEST: (*Quietly*) I think perhaps we'd better introduce ourselves, Laurence.

VAN DRAPER: Why, yes, of course. My name is Van Draper. Doctor Laurence Van Draper. This gentleman is Major Lindsay. He is, in fact, the father of the rather excitable young man you met in the village ... about ten minutes ago.

TEMPLE: I see.

GUEST: I believe I am correct in saying that my son gave you a letter ... A letter which he asked you to deliver to a certain Mr John Richmond?

TEMPLE: Yes. Yes, that's quite true.

GUEST: I should esteem it a favour if you would be good enough to give the letter to Doctor Van Draper.

There is a slight pause.

TEMPLE: I'm sorry, Major, but your son gave me explicit instructions that the letter was to be delivered to no one except Mr Richmond.

GUEST: I'm afraid your task will prove an extremely difficult one, sir. You see, there is no such person as ... John Richmond.

TEMPLE: (*Quietly*) No such person ...?

VAN DRAPER: Perhaps you'd better let me explain, Major. David Lindsay ... the young man who gave you the letter ... is unfortunately the victim of a rather peculiar ... what shall we say? ... mental condition?

STEVE: You mean that he isn't quite ...?

VAN DRAPER: He isn't quite responsible for certain of his actions. There's no real harm in the boy, in

71

	fact his condition is rapidly improving, but there are occasions … and tonight was one of them, I'm afraid … when he's a little er …
TEMPLE:	I understand. But tell me, how did you know about the letter?

There is a slight pause.

GUEST:	Mrs Moffat, at the little shop, rang through on the phone. She knows all about David's … weakness and understands.
TEMPLE:	Oh, yes. Yes, of course … Mrs Moffat. Here's the letter, doctor.
GUEST:	Thanks. I'll move my car out of the way so you can get by … I seem to have taken up all the road …
TEMPLE:	(*Amused*) You do, rather!
VAN DRAPER:	Goodnight …
STEVE:	(*Calling*) Goodnight!

TEMPLE's car moves forward.

The car finally gathers speed.

A long pause.

TEMPLE commences to chuckle.

STEVE:	(*Surprised*) Paul – what's the matter?
TEMPLE:	(*Amused*) Have you ever heard such a ridiculous story in all your life?
STEVE:	You mean … what the doctor said?
TEMPLE:	Doctor? He's no more a doctor than I am. The fellow didn't look like a doctor, and by Timothy he certainly didn't talk like one.
STEVE:	(*Puzzled*) Then … if you didn't believe his story, why did you give him the letter?

TEMPLE: I didn't, my dear. I gave him the postcards. Six delightful views of Inverdale. Two by moonlight.

FADE IN of music.

FADE DOWN of music.
A door opens.
ERNIE WESTON enters followed by TEMPLE, STEVE and MRS WESTON.
ERNIE is a pert, rather cheeky cockney.
MRS WESTON is buxom, north country and very homely.

MRS WESTON: I think you'll be very comfortable here. The Royal Gate isn't exactly what you might call palatial, but we do our best.

STEVE: Yes, this will do nicely, thanks.

ERNIE: I'll bring the other stuff up later. (*He is rather out of breath*) Where do I put this?

TEMPLE: It's all right … I'll see to that, old man.

MRS WESTON: Have you come far, sir?

TEMPLE: We left Edinburgh this morning, about ten.

ERNIE: Pretty good going … I expect you're feeling a bit peckish?

STEVE: Yes, we are rather.

MRS WESTON: If you'll follow me, ma'am, I'll show you the bathroom.

STEVE: Yes, all right. Shan't be long, darling!

TEMPLE: O.K.

The door opens and closes.

ERNIE: I'll pop down an' get the other stuff up, sir, an' then …

TEMPLE: No, just a minute. (*Conversationally*) Do you and your wife … er … run this place?

ERNIE: That's right, sir. Weston's the name. Ernie and Molly Weston. Been 'ere two years.

TEMPLE:	I see. (*Quickly*) Have you by any chance a man staying here called Richmond, John Richmond?
ERNIE:	(*Surprised*) Why, yes! Pal of yours?
TEMPLE:	No … but I'd like to have a word with him.
ERNIE:	Well, he's out at the moment. But he'll be in to dinner.
TEMPLE:	All right, I'll see him then. (*Offering a tip*) Here you are.
ERNIE:	Oh, thank you, sir. If you want anything special for dinner, just tell the missis!

The door closes.

TEMPLE commences to unpack.

He is whistling to himself.

After a pause the door opens.

STEVE:	(*Excited*) Paul, the most amazing thing has …
TEMPLE:	(*Interrupting*) I say … I say, what's all the excitement about?
STEVE:	Paul … who do you think I've seen?
TEMPLE:	I haven't the vaguest idea.
STEVE:	Iris Archer!
TEMPLE:	(*Amazed*) Iris! Here?
STEVE:	Yes, darling.
TEMPLE:	Don't be silly, Steve.
STEVE:	(*Seriously*) Darling, I'm not joking. I really have seen her. I was coming out of the bathroom when a door opened at the far end of the corridor … and out stepped Iris. Was I surprised!
TEMPLE:	Did she see you?
STEVE:	(*Thoughtfully*) I don't know … I have an idea she did …
TEMPLE:	But – but what happened?

74

STEVE: There's a staircase at the end of the corridor … before I could say anything, she disappeared.

TEMPLE: (*Thoughtfully*) M'm … that's certainly peculiar … But what would Iris be doing here? Besides – she's supposed to be on her way to South America.

STEVE: (*Quickly*) Paul!

TEMPLE: What?

STEVE: I've just remembered … That letter! Hadn't you better enquire about …

TEMPLE: I have … and there is a Mr John Richmond, after all.

There is a knock at the door.

The door opens.

ERNIE: I beg your pardon, sir, but I believe you wanted to see Mr Richmond. I met the gent on the stairs, sir, so I thought as how I'd better …

TEMPLE: Oh, yes. Please ask him in.

ERNIE: (*At the door*) This way, sir!

There is a slight pause.

STEVE: (*Amazed*) Why … why … Sir Graham!

TEMPLE: (*Staggered*) Sir Graham, what … what the devil are you doing here?

FORBES: (*Quietly*) There seems to be some mistake. My name is Richmond. John Richmond.

STEVE: (*Softly, still bewildered*) Richmond …

Suddenly and rather unexpectedly TEMPLE commences to chuckle.

TEMPLE: (*Amused*) Really, sir … we must beg your forgiveness! (*He is acting a little nonsensical*) By God, I've never seen anything like it … The same chin … The same nose … The

75

	same eyes … Why, he's just like old Forbes, the absolute 'spit' of old Forbes … (*Bewildered*) Well, I'm damned!
FORBES:	(*Irritated*) I say, what the devil is all this about? Who is this lady and gentleman?
ERNIE:	(*Puzzled*) This is the gent you wanted to see … Mr Richmond.
STEVE:	Oh, yes – that's all right. But you see we haven't met Mr Richmond before, and he's rather like a friend of ours, so naturally …
FORBES:	(*Curtly*) Very interesting, I'm sure. But unfortunately my time is valuable, so if you'll kindly …
TEMPLE:	Yes, of course. Of course. Permit me to introduce myself, my name is … (*Suddenly*) It's all right, Weston …
ERNIE:	(*Slowly*) We don't serve dinner after a quarter to …
TEMPLE:	(*Politely*) We shall bear that in mind.

The door closes.

A pause.

TEMPLE:	Sir Graham, I'm most terribly sorry … it was extremely stupid of us both …
FORBES:	That's all right! You covered it up well. But – but what the devil are you two doing here?
TEMPLE:	Well as …
FORBES:	(*Suddenly*) Yes! Yes, and there's another thing, Temple! You asked to see Mr John Richmond – I am John Richmond! So how on earth …
STEVE:	(*Quickly*) Paul – give Sir Graham the letter!
FORBES:	(*Seriously*) What letter?
TEMPLE:	A letter from a young man called Lindsay … David Lindsay.

FORBES:	(*Surprised*) For me?
TEMPLE:	Yes.
FORBES:	(*Puzzled*) I don't know anyone called David Lindsay. There must be some mistake.
STEVE:	(*Astonished*) You … don't … know anyone called Lindsay?
TEMPLE:	(*Chuckling*) This gets brighter and brighter! First of all I meet the delightful Mrs Moffat, then the excitable Mr Lindsay later …
FORBES:	(*Surprised*) Mrs Moffat? You mean the woman in the village?
TEMPLE:	That's right. The dark eyed beauty with a sister in Peckham.
FORBES:	(*Seriously, after a tiny pause*) How did you meet Mrs Moffat?
STEVE:	(*Wearily*) It's all right, darling, I'll tell him. We got lost, Sir Graham … and to make absolutely certain of getting on the right road …
TEMPLE:	I popped into Mrs Moffat's. Just as I was on the verge of leaving in barged the young fellow I was telling you about … David Lindsay. To cut a long story short he asked me if I was coming into Inverdale and whether I'd deliver a letter for him to a Mr John Richmond – who happened to be staying here … at The Royal Gate. Naturally, I agreed to do so. On the way here, however, two men stopped us. A man who called himself Dr Laurence Van Draper and another fellow – rather a military-looking chap – who claimed that he was a Major Lindsay. They told us a rather one-sided story about the young man being a bit silly, and more or less …

77

	demanded the letter. They were quite nice about things, but obviously meant business.
FORBES:	(*Eagerly*) But what happened?
STEVE:	Well, Paul happened to buy a packet of postcards – which fortunately Mrs Moffat popped into an envelope so when …
FORBES:	You don't mean to say that you gave them the postcards?
TEMPLE:	I'm afraid so.
FORBES:	Well, I'm damned! (*Suddenly*) Now listen, Temple, and this is most important … What was the young man like?
TEMPLE:	You mean Lindsay? Oh … he was about five foot … ten. Dark … Good looking … rather like John Mills, the film actor, except that his …
FORBES:	(*Excited*) My God, it's … Hammond all right … (*Amazed*) Noel Hammond … Now, of course, I understand why … (*Suddenly*) What's the matter?
STEVE:	(*Rather surprised*) Darling, what is it …?
TEMPLE:	(*Amazed, searching his pockets*) It's – It's the letter …
STEVE:	The letter …?
FORBES:	(*Softly, desperately*) Temple, you don't mean to say that …
TEMPLE:	(*Quietly*) It's gone!
STEVE:	Gone! But Paul, it couldn't possibly have gone unless …
FORBES:	You didn't make a mistake, Temple?
TEMPLE:	You mean – with the postcards? No. I had the letter when I arrived here. I'm absolutely certain of that. Someone must have taken it from me …

78

FORBES: That letter's important, Temple. Desperately
            important! We've got to get it back …

TEMPLE: Those men … Van Draper and the man who
            called himself Major Lindsay, they must have
            got in touch with someone … someone here
            … at The Royal Gate!

FORBES: Yes.

TEMPLE: (*Quietly*) Sir Graham, what's this all about?
            Why are you calling yourself John Richmond,
            and why …

FORBES: About two years ago, Temple, a man called
            John Hardwick wrote to the War Office
            concerning an invention of his, an invention
            which he called The Hardwick Screen. The
            Hardwick Screen was a system of camouflage
            for use on land. The War Office gave the
            screen a try out … and to cut a long story
            short … it was a terrible flop! The screen
            itself was all right, but the beam … or
            antidote as it were … a dismal failure.
            Without the beam, of course, the whole bag of
            tricks was a washout. Hardwick had a devil of
            a row with the War Office and returned to
            Scotland. (*He pauses*) After Hardwick
            returned to Scotland, however, the
            Intelligence people started taking an interest
            in the matter.

TEMPLE: (*Interested, but rather puzzled*) But why
            should the Intelligence people be interested in
            the screen, if the War Office had already
            turned it down?

FORBES: I'm glad you've asked that question, Temple
            … because it's the crux of the whole matter!
            For many years now the British Secret

	Service … and Scotland Yard for that matter … have realised that there existed in Europe one of the greatest independent espionage organisations of all time. An organisation under the direct control of one man … or woman … (*Dramatically*) Z4!!!
STEVE:	(*Softly*) Z4 …?
TEMPLE:	(*Slowly; shrewdly*) So you circulated a report that the test had been successful, knowing full well that under those circumstances Z4 was almost bound to contact Hardwick?
FORBES:	Exactly! But that wasn't all we did, Temple. A young fellow called Hammond – a brilliant research chemist and a member of the British Intelligence – had been interested in the possibility of Hardwick's Screen from the very first … He was also interested, like everyone else in the Secret Service, in the identity of Z4. Being a clever young devil, Hammond, or David Lindsay as he apparently called himself, discovered that Iris Archer – the actress – was a member of Z4's organisation.
STEVE:	Iris?
FORBES:	He played up to her like hell and before very long he found himself working side by side with … (*He stops*) What's that?

A knock is heard on the door.

After a slight pause the knock is repeated.

| STEVE: | There's someone at the door! |

The door is opened.

| TEMPLE: | No one's here! |
| FORBES: | There's a note on the floor – it looks as if it's … |

TEMPLE:	My God …!
FORBES:	What is it?
TEMPLE:	It's – It's the letter that … that Lindsay gave me … I recognise the envelope.
FORBES:	(*Excitedly*) Doesn't look as if it's been opened either …

FORBES tears open the envelope.

STEVE:	(*Softly*) It seems strange that it should be returned like this – unopened.
FORBES:	(*Excited*) Listen – Listen … to … this … "Identity of Z4 unknown … even by important members of organisation. Believe Z4 to be in Scotland and likely to contact headquarters within next three weeks. John Hardwick prisoner at Skerry Lodge …" (*He paused, obviously staggered*) My God, Temple, listen to this … (*Reading*) "Screen of definite value and importance. Beam almost perfected. Imperative Hardwick rescued. Noel Hammond."
TEMPLE:	My God, if Hardwick is on the right track, and according to Noel Hammond's report he most certainly is, then …
FORBES:	Then it's absolutely imperative that we get Hardwick away from Skerry Lodge!!!
STEVE:	Yes, but surely Noel Hammond's at Skerry Lodge so obviously …
FORBES:	(*Quietly*) Even if Hammond is still alive, which I very much doubt, he's not likely to be at Skerry Lodge, Steve.
STEVE:	(*Puzzled*) I don't understand.
TEMPLE:	(*Softly*) Sir Graham means that since they know about the letter they must obviously

	know that Hammond – or David Lindsay as they call him – is a British Agent.
STEVE:	Oh, yes. Yes, of course. (*Thoughtfully*) So, who were those men – the two that stopped us on the road?
FORBES:	One was obviously Laurence Van Draper, and the other man who called himself Major Lindsay was a gentleman by the name of Major Guest.
STEVE:	Then you know those people?
FORBES:	Oh, yes, we know them all right. The Intelligence people know every member of the organisation, with the unfortunate …
STEVE:	(*Interrupting*) But if they know them, then why don't they do something about it?
FORBES:	Because we're after bigger fish than Iris Archer, and Van Draper, and Major Guest, Steve! We're after the one person that really matters …Z4!
STEVE:	But who is Z4?
FORBES:	(*After a moment: quietly*) I don't know.
TEMPLE:	(*Softly*) Sir Graham …
FORBES:	Yes?
TEMPLE:	What sort of a place is this … Skerry Lodge?
FORBES:	Oh, it's rather like a medieval castle. It's built on the side of a small lake, Loch Aberford I believe they call it. (*After a moment*) Why do you ask?
TEMPLE:	(*Casually*) Oh … I was just thinking. Steve and I aren't very well known round here and I thought it might be quite a good idea if we …
FORBES:	(*Slowly*) If you – what –?
TEMPLE:	(*Quietly*) If we paid John Hardwick a visit …

A long pause.

FORBES: (*Slowly, thoughtfully*) Yes. Yes, quite a
                    good idea.

FADE IN of music.

Slow FADE DOWN of music.
FADE UP of a new scene.

VAN DRAPER: I tell you his name wasn't Lindsay – it was
                    Hammond! Noel Hammond of the British
                    Intelligence!

IRIS: I – I don't believe it!

GUEST: I'm afraid it's true, Iris.

IRIS: But – But it's unbelievable! I ran into
                    Lindsay almost two years ago! He had a
                    police record from here to Tokyo! I
                    checked up on him before I even
                    recommended him to Z4. (*Alarmed*)
                    Honestly, Laurence, I never even
                    suspected that …

VAN DRAPER: That's all right. Hammond was a clever
                    devil … he convinced us that he was on
                    the level too.

IRIS: What's going to happen?

VAN DRAPER: (*Politely*) To Mr Hammond?

GUEST: (*Suavely*) It's already happened, Iris – we
                    took care of Mr Hammond an hour ago.

IRIS: (*After a moment; softly*) I see.

GUEST: When did you arrive?

IRIS: Last night. (*After a pause*) Is everything
                    … all right?

GUEST: Perfectly. Now we're simply waiting for
                    … Z4.

IRIS: (*Amazed; quietly*) Waiting for Z4? You
                    mean waiting for instructions from Z4 …

VAN DRAPER: We mean … waiting … for Z4 …

IRIS: (*Laughing*) Don't be ridiculous! He's kept us in the dark so far, you don't think …

VAN DRAPER: This time Z4 is coming out into the open. He's got to …

IRIS: How do you know this?

GUEST: Mrs Moffat had a letter – almost two weeks ago.

VAN DRAPER: Iris …

IRIS: Yes?

VAN DRAPER: What does this Paul Temple business mean? Why is he staying at The Royal Gate?

IRIS: He's on holiday.

VAN DRAPER: Are you sure that … he's on holiday?

IRIS: (*Irritated*) Have we any reason to suspect otherwise?

VAN DRAPER: No, not at the moment, Iris, but if by … (*Suddenly*) What is it, Ben?

BEN: Mrs Moffat's here!

GUEST: (*Surprised*) What!

The door opens.

IRIS: Why, hello, Mrs Moffat!

A tiny pause.

VAN DRAPER: (*Quietly*) What's happened?

A second pause.

MRS MOFFAT: You've got to get Hardwick away …

VAN DRAPER: (*Surprised*) Why?

GUEST: (*Nervously*) What is it?

BEN: My God, don't say the …

IRIS: You've had instructions …?

MRS MOFFAT: Yes. (*After a tiny pause*) There's nothing to get alarmed about … only we've got to get Hardwick and the screen away from Skerry Lodge.

VAN DRAPER: (*Softly*) But … why?

MRS MOFFAT: Because of Paul Temple …

GUEST: (*Slightly puzzled*) Because … of Temple …

VAN DRAPER: I don't understand.

MRS MOFFAT: (*Slowly*) He's coming here …

GUEST: (*Astonished*) Here!

VAN DRAPER: (*Quietly*) How do you know this?

MRS MOFFAT: (*She is smiling*) Instructions … from Z4 …

BEN: And what's going to happen?

MRS MOFFAT: Van Draper and Guest can take Hardwick down to the chalet. Hold him there until you receive word from Ben.

BEN: And what the devil am I supposed to be doing while all this is going on?

MRS MOFFAT: Entertaining … Mr Temple.

BEN: (*Alarmed*) Entertaining … Temple!

MRS MOFFAT: When Temple arrives show him into the lounge and then go down to the basement.

VAN DRAPER: (*Alarmed*) My God … you don't want me to flood the place?

MRS MOFFAT: That's exactly what I do want you to do. Only make certain Temple is in the basement before the water reaches the first grid.

GUEST: (*Staggered*) Why … Why, they'll be trapped like rats …

BEN: (*Thoughtfully*) The idea's all right, if we can get Temple into the basement …

MRS MOFFAT: You'll get him there – if you use your head!

BEN: (*Thoughtfully*) Yes. Yes …

VAN DRAPER: (*Suddenly*) We'd better start packing, Guest – there's no time to lose.

BEN:	Just a minute! What the devil happens to me after … it's all over?
MRS MOFFAT:	You'll meet Iris at the junction near High Moorford. She'll bring you down to the chalet.
BEN:	O.K. (*To GUEST*) You'd better give me a hand with the pump, it takes a devil of a time to get it going.
GUEST:	Yes. Yes, all right.
IRIS:	Oh, Mrs Moffat …
MRS MOFFAT:	Well?
IRIS:	Laurence tells me that very soon we shall …
MRS MOFFAT:	We shall meet … Z4 …?
IRIS:	Yes. (*After a moment*) But how shall we recognise him?
MRS MOFFAT:	I shall recognise him, my dear.
IRIS:	Yes, but … how?
MRS MOFFAT:	By a quotation …
IRIS:	(*Surprised*) A quotation?

A pause.

MRS MOFFAT:	(*Slowly*) What was it Shakespeare said … about … travellers …? (*She chuckles*)

FADE IN of music.

Slow FADE DOWN of music.
CROSS FADE to the sound of a car.
After a short while the car suddenly brakes to a standstill.
The engine is switched off, and the car door opens.
There are footsteps on a gravel path.
There is a pause.

TEMPLE:	(*Quietly*) By Timothy, Sir Graham was certainly right when he called this place a mediaeval castle!

STEVE:	(*Rather nervously*) Darling, don't you think we ought to go round to the side of the house before …
TEMPLE:	Sssh!
STEVE:	What is it?
TEMPLE:	There's someone coming …
STEVE:	(*Surprised*) Did – did you ring the bell?
TEMPLE:	Yes. It's all right, Steve, don't get frightened.

The door opens.

BEN:	(*Rather more dignified*) Good evening, sir.
TEMPLE:	Good evening. I should like to see Mr Hardwick. My name is …
BEN:	Mr Hardwick is very busy just at the moment, sir, but if you'll step this way …
TEMPLE:	Thank you. Come along, darling.

The door closes.

There is a pause.

A second door opens.

BEN:	What name shall I say, sir?
TEMPLE:	Temple … Paul Temple …
BEN:	Thank you, sir.

The door closes.

STEVE:	(*Quickly, rather alarmed*) Paul … Paul, we shouldn't have come here …
TEMPLE:	(*Quietly*) It's all right, darling … (*He is obviously studying his surroundings*) I say, it's a pretty decent sort of place this … Certainly believes in doing himself well …
STEVE:	I didn't notice Sir Graham when we left the inn. I hope you told him we …
TEMPLE:	Sir Graham was telephoning … (*Suddenly*) Hardwick must be worth a packet by the look of things … just have a look at this picture …

	I'd like to bet a fiver it's a genuine … (*He stops*)
STEVE:	What is it?
TEMPLE:	Sh! (*A tiny pause*) He's coming back …

A slight pause.

The door opens.

BEN:	Mr Hardwick is extremely busy, sir, but if you'd care to step down to his laboratory then I think perhaps he might be able to spare you a …
TEMPLE:	Yes, of course. Come along, Steve!
BEN:	I should leave your things here, sir … you'll be able to pick them up on the way back. Allow me, madam!
STEVE:	Oh, thank you!

A slight pause.

A door opens.

BEN:	This way, sir.

The door closes.

A long pause.

A second door opens and closes.

It is heavy and rather solid.

There is a slight pause.

BEN:	In here, sir.
TEMPLE:	Thank you.

The door closes again.

STEVE:	Paul … I … don't like the look of this place.
TEMPLE:	(*Quietly*) No, I'm not exactly enamoured.

A pause.

STEVE:	What are you doing?
TEMPLE:	(*In the background*) I'm … trying … the door.
STEVE:	(*Alarmed*) Paul – Paul, what is it?

TEMPLE: (*Softly*) My God, Steve … we ought to have had more sense. (*Bitterly*) We ought to have had more sense!

TEMPLE is struggling with the door.

TEMPLE: M'm – we shan't get out of here in a hurry …

STEVE: But … But why have they done this? I – I don't understand …

TEMPLE: Obviously our visit wasn't entirely a surprise!

STEVE: (*Softly*) Can't we break the door down?

TEMPLE: Not this door, I'm afraid.

TEMPLE throws his weight against the door.

STEVE: Why is it padded at the foot …?

TEMPLE: (*Quietly*) I don't know …

STEVE: Paul!

TEMPLE: What is it?

STEVE: Oh. Oh, nothing …

TEMPLE: What is it, Steve?

STEVE: (*Puzzled*) Well – it seems silly but I thought I heard … (*Suddenly*) Paul – look! No! No! Near the ventilator!

TEMPLE: My God! (*Softly*) So that's what it is …

STEVE: They're – They're flooding the room …

Water can now be heard in the background rushing through one of the carefully placed ventilators.

TEMPLE throws his weight against the door again.

TEMPLE: Open the door! Open the door!

STEVE: (*Alarmed*) Paul … we've got to get out of here … we've got to get out of here …

TEMPLE: (*Banging against the door*) Open … the … door … (*Rather breathlessly*) It's no use, I'm afraid … we'll just have to wait!

A long pause.

STEVE: We'd … we'd better get that chair and … and …

TEMPLE: Frightened?
STEVE: Yes. Yes … I am … rather …
A pause.
TEMPLE: At this rate I should say that we've got about
            an hour. Possibly longer … It's difficult to
            tell. (*A tiny pause*) Cold?
STEVE: (*Obviously rather frightened*) Yes … a little
            …

A pause.
TEMPLE: Steve …
STEVE: Yes, darling?
TEMPLE: I'm – I'm terribly sorry about this business.
STEVE: Don't be silly, Paul … it … it just can't be
            helped … that's all.

A pause.
TEMPLE: There's nothing we can do … I'm afraid …
            except wait.
STEVE: I suppose this room's on the side of the lake,
            otherwise …
TEMPLE: (*Thoughtfully*) Yes. Yes, it must be … (*After
            a tiny pause*) It's funny, you know … I've
            often wondered how people reacted under
            circumstances like this … Somehow I've
            always thought … (*He stops; gently*) What is
            it, dear?
STEVE: (*Near to tears*) Nothing. I was thinking, that's
            all …
TEMPLE: (*After a tiny pause*) I'm sorry, Steve.
STEVE: (*Crying slightly*) It's … nothing.
TEMPLE: (*Suddenly angry with himself*) Good God,
            we're talking as if the whole business was
            over … and we were finished! We're not
            finished! We got ourselves into this mess and
            we're going to get out of it.

90

TEMPLE beats on the door again, pounding his fists on the panel.

TEMPLE: (*Shouting*) Hello there!

STEVE: It's no use, Paul.

TEMPLE: (*Still beating on the door*) Hello there! (*Thoughtfully*) I'm afraid the door is hopeless.

A tiny pause.

TEMPLE: We might be able to stop the water … but it's doubtful.

TEMPLE takes off his jacket.

TEMPLE: Hold this coat, Steve.

STEVE: But there's two grids, darling, even if you manage to stop one …

TEMPLE: (*Struggling with his jacket*) If we … stop one … we shall hold out longer … at any rate. (*Desperately*) My God, we shall have to be quick, Steve!

STEVE: (*Suddenly*) Paul!

TEMPLE: What is it?

STEVE: Didn't you hear anything?

TEMPLE: (*Thoughtfully*) No. No … the water seems to be gathering force, I shouldn't be surprised if …

STEVE: (*Suddenly*) Paul … listen!

Somewhere in the very distant background SIR GRAHAM FORBES can be heard.

FORBES: (*Shouting wildly*) Temple! Temple! Where are you? Temple, can you hear me? Temple!

TEMPLE: (*Suddenly and for the first time rather desperate*) My God, it's Forbes! We've got to make him hear us, Steve! (*Banging on the door*) Sir Graham! Open the door! Open … the … door! (*He continues to throw his weight against the door*) Sir Graham …

91

The sound of the water is now much louder and apparently nearer.

STEVE: We'll have to be quick, darling!

TEMPLE: (*Shouting*) Forbes! Forbes! (*Once again he throws his weight against the door. Desperately*) Get me that chair …

STEVE: What are you going to do …?

TEMPLE: There's a fanlight … perhaps if we smash it he'll hear us better.

There is the sudden smashing of glass.

STEVE: Darling … you've cut yourself.

TEMPLE: (*Almost frantic*) No … No, I'm all right! (*Shouting*) Forbes! Forbes!

FORBES: (*Much nearer*) Where the devil are you, Temple?

TEMPLE: We're at the end of the corridor! For God's sake be quick!

Suddenly there is the sound of footsteps.

FORBES: (*Shouting from the corridor*) Stand away from the door!

TEMPLE: Stand back, Steve!

There is a resounding crash, which is followed by several heavy blows on the door.

Suddenly the door gives way, and the splintering of wood is followed by a loud splash and a final rush of water.

FORBES: (*Staggered*) What on earth's happened?

TEMPLE: (*Excitedly*) We'll explain later … (*Suddenly*) For God's sake, let's get out of here!

FORBES: Look at Steve, she's going to faint!

STEVE: (*Weakly*) No … No. I'm … all right …

TEMPLE: (*Obviously taking hold of STEVE*) I've got her … (*Dramatically*) Lead the way, Sir Graham, lead the way …

FADE IN of music.

Slow FADE DOWN of music.
FADE SCENE.

CROSS FADE to the sound of a motor car.
It is travelling at a leisurely speed.

TEMPLE: It beats me how on earth you managed to find the place!

FORBES: Iris Archer told me – we've arrested her.

STEVE: Iris?

FORBES: Yes, she was in a car near the junction of High Moorford.

TEMPLE: And Hardwick?

FORBES: (*Obviously worried*) I don't know what's happened to Hardwick! But by God, we've got to find out, Temple! That's why we arrested Iris.

STEVE: Was Iris alone?

FORBES: No. There was a man with her called Collins. Ben Collins. You'll recognise him when you see him – he acted as the butler.

TEMPLE: Where are they now?

FORBES: I've had them both taken back to the inn. (*Suddenly*) Oh, by the way! Another friend of yours seems to have turned up …

TEMPLE: Oh? Who's that?

FORBES: A fellow called Bryant … Rex Bryant.

TEMPLE: (*Quietly*) Rex Bryant …?

STEVE: (*Surprised*) Rex Bryant!

TEMPLE: But what's he doing here?

FORBES: I haven't the vaguest idea! Apparently he arrived at The Royal Gate late last night. (*After a moment*) He's a newspaper reporter, isn't he?

TEMPLE: (*After a pause; thoughtfully*) Yes …

FADE UP of the car.
FADE the car completely.
FADE SCENE.

CROSS FADE to MRS WESTON.
She is obviously very distressed.
A door opens and closes.

FORBES: (*Surprised*) Hello, Mrs Weston!

STEVE: Is anything the matter?

TEMPLE: What seems to be the trouble?

MRS WESTON: Oh, sir! I can't understand it! He's never done this before. We've been married for nigh on sixteen years and Ernie hasn't so much as … (*She continues to cry*)

FORBES: But – But what's the matter, Mrs Weston?

MRS WESTON: It's Ernie, sir … he's … he's …

STEVE: Now come along, Mrs Weston – pull yourself together and tell us what's happened!

FORBES: Is your husband ill or something?

MRS WESTON: Oh, no, sir! It's – it's not that, sir. He's disappeared!

FORBES: (*Amazed*) Disappeared!

STEVE: Oh, but he can't have disappeared!

TEMPLE: (*Quietly*) When did you last see your husband?

MRS WESTON: Last night, sir … just after one of our guests arrived. We'd locked up for the night and was more or less getting ready for bed, as you might say, when Ernie suddenly took it into his head to go for a walk.

TEMPLE: Was he perfectly all right; I mean – in quite a good humour?

MRS WESTON: Oh, yes … he appeared to be, sir.

REX BRYANT arrives.

He is very bright and cheerful.

REX: Hello, everybody! Hello, Temple!

TEMPLE: Oh, hello, Bryant! How are you?

REX: I'm fine!

STEVE: We didn't expect to see you in this part of the world, Rex!

REX: You know the newspaper game, Steve! Here today and … (*Surprised*) Hello! Hello, Mrs Weston! Why the tears?

FORBES: It's Mr Weston – he apparently went out last night about eleven o'clock and hasn't been seen since.

REX: Good heavens! (*To MRS WESTON*) Was that your husband, Mrs Weston – the cheerful little chap who showed me to my room?

MRS WESTON: Yes, sir.

REX: Well, I shouldn't worry about him – he looked as if he could take care of himself.

STEVE: Yes, don't worry, my dear … he'll turn up all right.

REX: I'll see you later, Temple! I want to have a talk with you.

TEMPLE: Yes. Yes, all right, Bryant.

MRS WESTON: Here's your key, Mrs Temple …

STEVE: Thank you.

MRS WESTON: Oh, an' Mr Richmond – there's someone in your room! A gentleman who said 'is name was Inspector Carter an' two other …

FORBES: Yes, that's all right, Mrs Weston! (*Quietly*) Come along, Temple …

95

FADE SCENE.

FADE IN of IRIS.
She is annoyed and exasperated.

IRIS: For goodness sake don't keep on asking the same stupid question.

TEMPLE: Where have they taken John Hardwick?

IRIS: I tell you I don't know!

BEN: What right have you got to bring us here? Who the devil are you anyway?

FORBES: Now listen to me, Miss Archer, I'm a very determined man, and just at the moment I'm very determined to find out where they've taken John Hardwick!

IRIS: I've told you – I don't know!

BEN: (*Overwrought*) Leave us alone ... for God's sake ... leave us alone!!!!

STEVE: (*Quietly*) Iris, how did you know that Paul and I were going to visit Skerry Lodge?

BEN: (*Exasperated*) Mrs Moffat told us!

IRIS: (*Angry*) Shut up you fool!

TEMPLE: (*Quietly*) So Mrs Moffat told you ... Go on, Ben ...

IRIS: (*Desperately*) Keep your mouth shut, you damn fool, or ...

TEMPLE: Go on, Ben ...

BEN: She came to the house and ... told us that she had ... received instructions from ...

IRIS: Ben ... for God's sake keep your mouth shut!

TEMPLE: That she had received instructions from Z4 ...

BEN: Yes.

TEMPLE: How did Mrs ... (*Quietly; surprised*) Steve ... Steve, what is it?

A tiny pause.

STEVE: (*Staring; quietly*) Darling, look at that cupboard …

TEMPLE: What's the matter with it?

STEVE: I mean … on the floor. There's something trickling between …

IRIS: (*Softly*) It's blood!!!!

TEMPLE: (*Quietly*) Open the cupboard door, Sir Graham.

There is a slight pause.

STEVE: Paul … you don't think …?

TEMPLE: (*Softly*) Open the cupboard, Sir Graham!

The cupboard door opens and the body of ERNIE WESTON is discovered.

STEVE utters a terrific shriek as the body falls.

FORBES: My God … it's Weston … He's dead!!!

TEMPLE: He's dead … all right.

STEVE: (*Very distressed*) Oh, Paul … how horrible … how horrible … I … I feel faint.

FORBES: Look out, Temple, she's going to faint!!!

STEVE: (*Weakly*) No. No … I'm all right.

TEMPLE: Sit down, dear.

A pause.

FORBES: There's something in his hand. It looks to me like … Yes, it is … it's a watch chain …

TEMPLE: Let me have a look … (*After a pause*) I've … I've seen that chain somewhere before … It seems as … (*Suddenly*) What is it, Steve?

STEVE: The watch chain … I … I know who it belongs to …

FORBES: (*Excitedly*) Who?

STEVE: Why … Bryant, of course … Rex Bryant!

FADE IN of music.

Slow FADE DOWN of music.

FADE SCENE.

FADE UP ALEC's voice.

ALEC: Is there anything else I can get you, sir?

TEMPLE: No, I don't … (*Suddenly*) Oh, hello, darling.
           I'm just having a drink. What would you like?

STEVE: Nothing for me, Paul – not at the moment.

TEMPLE: Here we are …

ALEC: Oh, thank you, sir.

A pause.

STEVE: Have you seen Sir Graham?

TEMPLE: Not since this morning – he promised to meet
           me here at four o'clock.

STEVE: You know that Iris broke down and
           confessed?

TEMPLE: About them taking Hardwick down to the
           chalet? Yes. Rex Bryant tells me that Sir
           Graham's been on the lake since six o'clock
           this morning.

STEVE: (*Puzzled*) Paul, is Rex Bryant mixed up in this
           business?

TEMPLE: Well, I hardly think he's in Scotland for the
           good of his health, Steve.

STEVE: But what reason does he give for being here?
           I mean, he's so frightfully evasive.

TEMPLE: I had a chat with Bryant last night – quite a
           long chat. He apparently got wind of the John
           Hardwick story and came up to Scotland to
           see what it was all about.

STEVE: Did you mention the watch chain?

TEMPLE: (*Thoughtfully*) Yes …

STEVE: What did he say?

TEMPLE: He claims to have lost it soon after he arrived
           – apparently he had a word with Mrs Weston
           about it.

STEVE:	Well, all I can say is, if Rex … (*Suddenly*) Oh, hello, Mrs Weston! Just going down into the village?
MRS WESTON:	Yes, there are one or two things I must see to and … and I feel so much better when my mind's occupied.
STEVE:	Yes. Yes, I expect you do.
TEMPLE:	(*Quietly*) Mrs Weston, I'm awfully sorry to trouble you, but tell me … did Mr Bryant speak to you about a watch chain?
MRS WESTON:	(*Surprised*) About a watch chain?
TEMPLE:	Yes, apparently he lost one soon after he arrived.
MRS WESTON:	No. No, he said nothing to me about – not that I can recall.
STEVE:	You're probably confused, darling.
TEMPLE:	(*Laughing*) I think I must be!
MRS WESTON:	I'll have a word with Alec about it …

A pause.

STEVE:	Well, what do you make of that?
TEMPLE:	I think … (*Changing his mind*) I think this is Sir Graham!
FORBES:	Hello, Temple!
STEVE:	You look tired, Sir Graham!
FORBES:	And I feel tired, Steve! Whose drink is this?
TEMPLE:	Mine.
FORBES:	Well, here goes! (*He drinks*)
TEMPLE:	(*Amused*) You see the glint in his eye, Steve! Beneath that tired countenance lurks – yes, positively lurks a smile of self-satisfaction! The Chief Commissioner is delighted with himself!
STEVE:	What happened? Did you find the chalet?

99

FORBES:	(*Pleased*) At four o'clock this afternoon. We rescued Hardwick and we arrested Guest and Van Draper …
TEMPLE:	But not Z4 …
FORBES:	No, Temple … not Z4.
TEMPLE:	I suppose you've still got someone up at Skerry Lodge?
FORBES:	Yes – and I've still got a man watching Mrs Moffat's place, although I've given him strict instructions to keep in the background.
TEMPLE:	We were just talking about Rex Bryant, Sir Graham, when you arrived.
FORBES:	I'm not at all happy about Bryant. After all, don't forget we found his watch chain on Ernie Weston …
TEMPLE:	But that isn't necessarily an indication that Bryant was implicated – in Weston's murder I mean.
FORBES:	But good heavens, Temple, he must be mixed up in this business, otherwise how the devil did Weston get hold of his watch chain in the first place?
TEMPLE:	He helped himself to it!
STEVE:	You mean that Ernie Weston was just …
TEMPLE:	Just an ordinary common little pickpocket.
FORBES:	(*Faintly exasperated*) Then if Weston was just an ordinary common little pickpocket and didn't have a row with Rex Bryant – who the devil killed him?
TEMPLE:	Z4.
FORBES:	(*Irritated*) But why? In heaven's name … why?

TEMPLE: (*Quietly*) Your guess is as good as mine, Sir Graham.

A slight pause.

FORBES: (*Softly*) But what is your guess, Temple?

TEMPLE: (*Earnestly*) My guess is this. The moment I arrived at the inn, Weston went through my pockets and found the letter that Lindsay – or Hammond if you like – had given me. Later, realising that the letter might possibly be of some personal value to me, he returned it … You remember – the letter was pushed under the door!

FORBES: Yes. Yes, but that still doesn't explain why he was murdered!

TEMPLE: Doesn't it?

FORBES: What do you mean, Temple?

TEMPLE: I mean simply this, Sir Graham. After he had returned the letter the poor devil obviously mentioned the fact to someone, and that someone … happened to be Z4. Naturally Z4 wanted the letter before it got into your hands … it was, in fact, absolutely imperative that Hammond's message shouldn't reach you. And yet Ernie Weston, after having had possession of the letter, had calmly returned it. By Timothy, you can imagine how Z4 felt about it …

FORBES: My God, yes … it's certainly a motive. It's certainly a motive.

STEVE: (*Suddenly*) But Weston couldn't have known anything at all about Z4, or he'd have understood the message!

TEMPLE: Exactly.

FORBES:	Look here, Temple, supposing Bryant started questioning Weston about the watch chain. Weston got a bit nervous, began to think Bryant was some sort of a police officer, and without thinking started on about the letter. Bryant would naturally put two-and-two together and …
STEVE:	(*Excitedly*) Exactly!
TEMPLE:	(*Faintly amused; almost dismissing the subject*) Well, it's quite a theory, Sir Graham. (*Calling*) Alec!
ALEC:	Yes, sir?
TEMPLE:	Bring two more dry Martinis.
ALEC:	Yes, sir.
STEVE:	Make it three, darling!
TEMPLE:	Sorry, Alec! (*Calling*) Three, Alec!
ALEC:	(*In the background*) Yes, sir.
FORBES:	I see the Golden Clipper had a pretty rough trip the other day. What was it like when you came across?
STEVE:	Perfect. We enjoyed every minute of it, didn't we, Paul?
TEMPLE:	Every minute.
FORBES:	I wish I could get away for a month or so. Never been to the States.
STEVE:	You'd like it.
FORBES:	Oh, well, we might think about it in a couple of years. Always wanted to travel. As Mrs Moffat would say: "What was it Shakespeare said about travellers?"

There is a pause.
The pause is long and obviously significant.

STEVE:	What is it, darling?

TEMPLE:	(*Extremely serious*) Sir Graham ... Mrs Moffat said that to you ... "What was it ... Shakespeare said ... about travellers?" ...?
FORBES:	(*Puzzled*) Why ... why, yes.
TEMPLE:	(*Almost desperate*) When? When did she say it?
FORBES:	Why, the first time I went into the shop ... (*Anxiously*) Good Lord, Temple, what the devil is it?
TEMPLE:	By Timothy, what a fool ... what an utter damn fool ...
STEVE:	Darling! Darling, what is it?
TEMPLE:	Don't you see! Don't you see! Mrs Moffat said exactly the same thing to me ... "What was it Shakespeare said about travellers?" If I'd given the right answer, or if you'd given it, Sir Graham ... She'd have thought we ... we were Z4!
FORBES:	(*Staggered*) My God ... you mean ... that's the password ...?
TEMPLE:	(*Thoughtfully*) What was it Shakespeare said ... about ... travellers ...? "Travellers ne'er did lie – though fools at home condemn 'em." Though fools at home condemn ... (*Desperately*) If only I'd thought of it, Sir Graham ... If only I'd thought of it!

FADE IN of music.
FADE DOWN music.
FADE SCENE.

FADE IN of FORBES speaking.

FORBES:	(*Softly*) What time is it, Temple?
TEMPLE:	I make it about seven-twenty; I don't know whether my watch is right or not.

103

STEVE:	Yes, that's about right, darling.
FORBES:	Good Heavens, we've been here about two hours …
MRS MOFFAT:	(*Angry*) And how much longer do ye intend staying here? Hanging about like a lot of lost sheep!
FORBES:	(*Quietly*) I think you know how long we intend staying here, Mrs Moffat – until Z4 arrives.
MRS MOFFAT:	Then for God's sake let's go into the shop, we can't all stay in here … If you don't get some air into this parlour I shall pass out on ye …
STEVE:	It is pretty close, Sir Graham.
FORBES:	Yes, but we can see the door from here without being noticed … Besides the shop must appear empty otherwise … (*He stops*)
STEVE:	What is it?
TEMPLE:	Sh!

A pause.

The shop door opens.

The bell is heard.

There is a pause.

STEVE:	(*Softly; excited*) Paul … Paul, it's Rex Bryant!
FORBES:	(*Extremely nervous*) You know what to do, Mrs Moffat. Now don't forget the quotation, because if there's any funny business …
TEMPLE:	(*Softly*) He's waiting, Mrs Moffat …

A pause.

MRS MOFFAT:	Good evening.
REX:	(*Brightly*) Oh, good evening.

MRS MOFFAT: What can I get ye?

REX: Well, as a matter of fact, I want some razor blades. Got any Pride of the Regiment?

MRS MOFFAT: No … I'm afraid … I haven't. (*Her words are almost mechanical. She is studying Bryant, rather than taking note of what he is saying*)

REX: Good Lord, you should always stock Pride of the Regiment. Wouldn't shave with anything else! Makes your face as smooth as a baby's … (*He stops*) I say, old girl, you'll know me the second time, an' no mistake …

MRS MOFFAT: You've been in here before … haven't you?

REX: (*Puzzled*) Yes … once or twice …

MRS MOFFAT: Where do you come from … now?

REX: (*Very breezy; imitating her*) Where do I come from … now? I'm from Chelsea, Mrs Moffat. Gay old Chelsea … where girls are girls, and men … well, that's a moot point.

MRS MOFFAT: Chelsea? That's a long way …

REX: Yes.

MRS MOFFAT: I've a married sister in London. Peckham, I believe. Is there a place called Peckham?

REX: (*Rather quietly*) Yes. There is a place called Peckham.

MRS MOFFAT: (*With a sigh*) It must be a wonderful thing to travel. Often I wish I had the time … an' the money of course. What was it Shakespeare said about travellers …?

REX: Don't ask me, lady! Ethel M. Dell is more
                       in my line! Sorry you're out of razor
                       blades!

The door opens and closes.

The bell rings.

FADE AWAY from the shop to the back parlour.

FORBES: (*Staggered*) Well, I'm damned!

STEVE: (*Amazed*) Then … Then Rex Bryant isn't
                       …

TEMPLE: Sh!

FORBES: (*Quickly*) There's someone else!

The door opens and the bell is heard.

There is a pause.

STEVE: Oh, it's only Mrs Weston!

FORBES: Now what the devil does she want?

FADE from the parlour to the shop.

MRS WESTON: Good evening, Mrs Moffat.

MRS MOFFAT: Oh, good evening, Mrs Weston. Shocking
             weather!

MRS WESTON: (*Shaking her raincoat*) I can't remember a
             worse winter than this, and that's the truth.
             We seem to have had nothing but rain
             since August.

MRS MOFFAT: I was sorry to hear about Ernie … it must
             have been a dreadful shock to ye?

MRS WESTON: (*With a sigh*) I don't suppose anyone will
             ever know just how much I miss him, Mrs
             Moffat. There are times when I find
             myself … (*Suddenly*) Oh, well. Now what
             was it I came in for? Really, my memory!
             I was wondering if you had some sort of a
             suitcase I could borrow? I'm thinking of
             going down to my sister's for a short while

106

... my married sister that is ... and the only case I have is an old ...

MRS MOFFAT: Yes, I think I can help you. You won't want to take the case straight away, I suppose?

MRS WESTON: Oh, no, there's no hurry.

MRS MOFFAT: I'll have the boy drop it in tomorrow morning.

MRS WESTON: That would do nicely.

MRS MOFFAT: Is it a long journey you'll be taking?

MRS WESTON: Yes, I suppose it is really ... Hove.

MRS MOFFAT: Hove?

MRS WESTON: Yes, it's near Brighton. Have you ever been there?

MRS MOFFAT: (*Nervously*) No. No, I'm afraid I haven't. There aren't many places I have been to tell the truth, Mrs Weston. Often thought I'd like to travel though; providing of course I had time an' money ... (*After a slight hesitation*) What was it Shakespeare said ... about travellers ...?

A pause.

MRS WESTON: (*Seriously*) He said ... "Travellers ne'er did lie ... though fools at home condemn 'em". Travellers ... ne'er ... did ... lie, Mrs Moffat.

MRS MOFFAT: Why, Mrs Weston, you mean that <u>you</u> and ...

MRS WESTON: Now listen! And listen carefully! These are your instructions. A car will leave High Moorford tomorrow morning at precisely 8.40 ... you will proceed immediately to your ...

107

A door is thrown open and MRS WESTON turns with a sudden start of astonishment.

MRS WESTON: My God, what's this?

TEMPLE: (*Shouting*) Drop that gun! Drop it!!!

FORBES: (*Staggered*) Good God, Temple … this is Mrs Weston!!! You don't mean to say …

TEMPLE: Permit me to introduce you to the leader of the greatest espionage organisation in Europe. (*Dramatically*) Z4!!!!

FADE IN of music.
Slow FADE DOWN of music.
FADE completely.

FADE IN gradually the voices of SIR GRAHAM, STEVE and PAUL TEMPLE.

STEVE: More coffee, Sir Graham?

FORBES: No thank you, Steve. Good gracious, is that clock right? I must be making a move!

STEVE: I'll ring for Pryce.

FORBES: You still haven't told me, Temple, why you suspected Mrs Weston.

TEMPLE: Well, in the first place she was always at the inn and therefore in a position to overhear most of our conversations. And secondly, she was the most obvious person for Weston to confide in about the letter.

STEVE: You mean that he told his wife about it without realising that she was Z4?

TEMPLE: Exactly. Although of course it wasn't quite so simple as that at the time. I knew he'd told <u>someone</u> about the letter, and I knew that someone was definitely Z4 … But it might have been an unknown person or possibly Rex Bryant. Now if it was

Bryant, I reflected, then obviously Weston must be on fairly friendly terms with him … Bryant must in fact know that he was in the habit of helping himself to other people's possessions – and yet Bryant had obviously been puzzled by the loss of his watch chain …

FORBES: I must confess I thought the watch chain a rather obvious 'plant' – if I hadn't have done so I'd have arrested Bryant on the spot.

STEVE: I suppose you've read Rex Bryant's account of all this in The London Evening Post?

FORBES: (*Laughing*) What an imagination! (*After a moment*) Oh, well – see you both next week. Now don't forget … Thursday. Carol's looking forward to it.

TEMPLE: (*Laughing*) Well, Steve's talking about going away for another holiday, Sir Graham.

FORBES: (*Amazed*) Well, you've certainly earned it … Goodbye, Steve!

STEVE: Goodbye, Sir Graham!

A pause.
The door closes.

TEMPLE: Well, my sweet?

STEVE: (*With a sigh*) It's nice to be home again, Paul.

TEMPLE: (*Amused*) Does that mean you'd like to go away for a few weeks?

STEVE: Yes, darling. Somewhere tranquil and quiet and … Do you know, Paul – I've got quite a fancy for Cornwall!

TEMPLE: (*Politely interested*) Cornwall?
STEVE: Yes, I don't think anything very exciting
            could possibly happen in Cornwall, do you,
            darling?
TEMPLE: (*After a moment: thoughtfully*) I wonder …
FADE IN of closing music.

THE END

Potting Paul Temple

Francis Durbridge, author of *Send for Paul Temple*, explains how he has made an hour's show of an eight-week serial.

During the spring of 1938 the BBC presented the first Paul Temple serial play, *Send for Paul Temple*. This play ran for eight weeks, and played for exactly one hundred and ninety-nine minutes! On Monday the BBC are repeating *Send for Paul Temple*, but on this occasion it will be broadcast as a complete radio play lasting for – yes, believe it or not – sixty minutes!

Since *Send for Paul Temple* was the first serial play to be turned into a novel after having been originally written for the radio, it is perhaps appropriate that Monday's broadcast will be the very first time that an eight weeks' serial has been condensed into a single performance!

In this brief article, however, I am not going to attempt to explain in detail how to condense a play lasting nearly three-and-a-half-hours into a programme of sixty minutes! Nor have I any intention of describing the mental agony of the author when scenes which have probably taken weeks to write and devise suddenly fall a victim of the blue pencil. But the first essential in this 'potting' process is to reconcile yourself to the fact that, if there is a particular scene which you are anxious – at all cost – to retain in the final script, you can bet your marmalade radio that this is the very scene which the producer is equally intent upon cutting.

In the original version of *Send for Paul Temple* there were sixteen principal characters, but in the abridged version only twelve remain. However, apart from Paul Temple himself, we still have Steve, Sir Graham Forbes, Chief-Inspector Dale, Diana Thornley, Dr Milton, our old friend Miss Parchment, and of course 'The Knave of Diamonds'. Naturally a great many of the scenes which proved effective when the play was presented as a serial have had to be partly re-written: this has been done not merely to condense the story, but because when a serial is presented as a complete broadcast one can achieve the effect of tension, the 'to-be-continued-next-week' feeling only by carefully avoiding any form of anti-climax.

Although a great many of the incidental episodes have been cut out of the original play, *Send for Paul Temple* is still essentially a play of mystery and thrills, so listeners must not imagine that the abridged version is merely a perfectly straight forward detective story.

Not a bit of it! Paul Temple may have only sixty minutes at his disposal, but I think you will find that quite a lot can happen in sixty minutes.

Radio Times

Printed in Great Britain
by Amazon

33946520R00074